D0275479

Running Against the Tide

Running Against the Tide

Joanna Barnden

ROBERT HALE · LONDON

© Joanna Barnden 2013
First published in Great Britain 2013

ISBN 978-0-7198-0740-4

Robert Hale Limited
Clerkenwell House
Clerkenwell Green
London EC1R 0HT

www.halebooks.com

The right of Joanna Barnden to be identified as author
of this work has been asserted by her in accordance with
the Copyright, Designs and Patents Act 1988

2 4 6 8 10 9 7 5 3 1

Typeset in 11/16½ Palatino
Printed in Great Britain by the MPG Books Group,
Bodmin and King's Lynn

Chapter One

The River Thames, June 1800

'The new docks will make all the difference to trade,' Ginny Marcombe said earnestly, gesturing around the crowded Thames from her vantage point on a boat in the middle of the swirling water. 'It should cut our operating costs by at least twenty per cent shouldn't it, Father?'

'If you say so, Ginny.' Josiah looked down at her fondly before turning back to the two merchants at their side. 'My daughter is the brains of our business, you know.'

The older man looked a little startled at this and stared at Ginny, clearly trying to see what a slip of a girl was doing in the cut-throat world of shipping. Ginny smiled at him sweetly – she was used to this reaction – but Josiah wasn't going to let it go.

'Don't be deceived by her feminine charms, Mr Johnson. Under that pretty face my Ginny has the mind of a man. She's the son I never had and she's going to do Marcombe's Shipping proud, right, girl?'

'Right, Father.'

Ginny drew herself up as tall as she could, wanting to be worthy of her father's high opinion of her. She knew that many people in the business thought Josiah was mad to put his trust in her, but she also knew that they were wrong. Ever since her mother's birthing-fever six years ago had made it clear that she would bear no sons, Ginny had worked harder than any boy to learn her father's trade.

Her two younger sisters had spent their time on music and art and embroidery, but Ginny was handier with a telescope than a needle, and more at home on a boat than sitting at a piano. Sometimes her mother would berate her father for 'spoiling her marriage prospects with all this education' but Josiah would just laugh.

'Ginny will have the finest marriage in the city, Eliza, my love. They'll be queuing up for her hand, won't they, lass?'

And Ginny was always forced to nod and smile for it was true – now she was eighteen there were plenty of young man keen to marry her. The younger Mr Johnson, looking round the little boat with strange eagerness, was one of them and she wasn't stupid enough to think he liked her soft, dark-blonde curls, or her deep brown eyes. He just wanted a place in her father's much-admired shipping business and Ginny had yet to meet a man who, in her eyes, merited a share in that.

'It's a new century!' Josiah proclaimed dramatically now. 'It's time to embrace change and move forward in a spirit of optimism and adventure.'

The two Mr Johnsons murmured approval of these worthy sentiments, wobbling a little as they shifted from foot to foot. For they were all on a lighter – a long, flat-bottomed boat normally designed to unload goods from the trading vessels moored in the Thames. This one had been unloading her father's latest import of coffee and sugar when Josiah had ambushed the young lighterman and insisted they were taken along too.

'Nothing like getting in with the workmen to really

understand the business,' he'd beamed, helping Ginny aboard and waving the merchants to follow.

Ginny had almost laughed out loud at their surprise at actually being asked to step on board one of the boats that made them their money. At times like this she loved her enthusiastic, unconventional father more than ever.

Ginny looked out across the crowded river towards the new buildings of the West India Docks just starting to rise above the Stepney Marshes. Josiah – and with him, Ginny – had been intimately involved in much of the planning of this brave venture designed to take some of the shipping off the bulging Thames and, oh, how it needed it! Ginny considered the lines of trade ships at anchor in the middle of the big river; the 'roads' of barges, stacked perilously high with goods, and the hundreds of smaller vessels expertly steering their way between them, catching the tides and fighting the winds that made this part of the river a constant danger to the unwary.

Her eye was caught by the young lighterman battling with his long paddles to steer their own vessel. As she watched, he ran nimbly along the edge of the boat, treading along the narrow gunnel as if it were a rambling meadow pathway. To one side of him he faced a nasty fall into the cargo hold where her father's coffee lay in spiky casks, and to the other the dark, swirling waters of the river. By the look of his broad back and firm arms he would be a good swimmer, but few men could fight the malice of the vicious current known as the Thames tunnel which ran just below the surface, ready to snatch any souls it could.

Ginny shivered. How did he live with such danger day in day out? He looked barely older than she and yet he carried himself with a captivating assurance. As she watched, he turned to head back her way and their eyes met. Ginny felt her heart start to beat faster and forced herself to hold his gaze as he approached. To her left, Josiah was excitedly telling the Johnsons all about the new business opportunities the Docks would open up, but for once she wasn't sharing his enthusiasm. Summoning up all her courage, she took a couple of steps away from her father and spoke to the young man.

'Is this your boat?'

'It is, ma'am. I inherited it from my Grandfather.'

'It's very nice.' Nice? She sounded like a fool. Hastily she tried again. 'Are you looking forward to the new docks?'

He tipped his head on one side.

'I'm not so sure about that yet, miss. I can see how it'll be good for shipping, and it might make for less danger out here on the river, but I'll admit that I'm scared for the future of my own trade.'

Ginny stared at him in dismay. He was right: if more ships could dock up to the land there would be less call for boats like this to ferry their goods in.

'I'm so sorry. I never thought of that.'

The lighterman rushed to reassure her.

'I'm sure it'll be fine. There will still be plenty needing our services for many a year yet and, if not, I'll find something new. Can't stand in the way of progress, can you?'

'No, I . . .'

It was exactly what Ginny felt herself but, unlike this man, this particular change could only bring her increased prosperity. She was about to ask him more, but a shout from a nearby boat called him to his duties and she returned to hers, newly thoughtful.

'We're looking to commission two new boats next year,' Josiah was saying. 'Ginny's secured very favourable terms with the boatyard and—'

'What design?'

'Sorry?' Josiah peered over at young Nathan Johnson who had spoken for the first time since they'd stepped on board the boat.

'What design are you planning to commission? It's just that I'm very interested in boats and there are some amazing new ideas coming through that could make all the difference to the speed and efficiency of the cargoes.'

'There are?' Josiah looked at the young man with new respect. 'Ginny. What do we know about these new designs?'

Ginny flushed.

'I'll look into it, Father.'

'Perhaps Nathan could help.'

Nathan was nodding keenly and his father, sensing a way into Josiah's favour, began boasting loudly about his son's knowledge.

'Perhaps you'd like to come to dinner and talk further. This evening?'

The older Mr Johnson shoved his son in the back and Nathan gabbled a hasty acceptance.

'Excellent. I'm sure you young people will have lots to talk about.'

Ginny felt her heart sink. She knew exactly what her father was up to and now that his enthusiasm for innovation had been caught by Nathan's ideas, she could see him making plans for their future together already.

Nathan's father shoved him again so that he tottered on the boat and staggered against Ginny.

'Oh, I'm so sorry.'

The two older men laughed knowingly and Ginny flushed, but a glance at Nathan showed her that he was as embarrassed as she, so she softened her ready guard and allowed herself to assess him. Nathan was tall and thin, but his clothes fitted him well and he held himself firmly. His nose was a little long and his mouth a little small, but she was far from perfect herself. Was this, then, the man she would marry?

Her eyes slid back to the lighterman. They were approaching the docks now and he was concentrating hard on navigating them safely into shore. Oblivious of her attention, she was free to watch his lithe, strong body as he leaned on the paddles, guiding them safely through the swirling tides. Something about his sense of purpose was very arresting but he belonged to a different world from her. And yet, hadn't her own father risen from a lowly merchant himself? And wasn't he defying convention to teach his daughter the shipping business? Might he not, then, be prepared to consider an unusual marriage for her too?

Ginny's cheeks flushed at her presumptuous thoughts and she forced herself to take her father's arm as the boat bumped in towards the shore. Josiah looked down at her fondly and patted her hand.

'Steady there!' the lighterman called up. 'Docking now.' His voice was thick with the Wapping burr but had a lilting quality Ginny liked. 'That's us ashore now, sirs, miss.'

He tipped his cap at her and she inclined her head a little, longing to do more to acknowledge his skill.

'Good work, man,' Josiah boomed. The lighterman had leapt ashore and was throwing a gangplank against the grimy side of the boat. 'What's your name?'

'Edward, sir. Edward Allerdice.'

Ginny stored it away.

'Well, Edward, here's a shilling for your trouble and mind you get my passengers ashore safely. They're precious – my Ginny especially.'

He nodded at his daughter and Edward leapt to her side, offering his hand. She glanced at it, tempted to seize it in a most unladylike way. Seeing her hesitation he hastily wiped it on his trousers.

'I'm sorry, miss. It's a grubby business this one.'

'Oh that doesn't worry me in the slightest.'

Ginny quickly took his hand before she offended him. It was large and warm and rough with blisters. His fingers clasped hers and she moved slowly – very slowly – down the gangplank, feeling safe in his grip. All too soon she was on the dock and had to let go. As she pulled away, however, she saw something on her palm: blood.

'Oh!' She stared at it, then at the young man from whom it had come. 'Are you all right?'

'Oh miss, I'm so sorry.'

He looked round for a cloth but her concern was all for him.

'You're bleeding.'

'Ay.' Seeing her horror, he smiled. It lit up his face. 'Hey now, don't you go worrying about that. It's just a blister burst.'

'Will it heal?'

'Will it heal? Chance'd be a fine thing. I'd have to stop rowing for them to heal and I could hardly do that, could I?'

'No, I . . .'

He softened.

'It's all right you know. I'm used to it. Goes with the trade.'

'I suppose so.'

'Virginia!' her father called but she was mesmerized.

'I have herbs that could help,' she offered.

Ginny had discovered the healing properties of herbs from the skilled old lady hired to ease her mother through the fever that had gripped her body after giving birth to little Charlotte.

Ginny's sharp brain had absorbed information fast and she'd carried on the lady's good work for some time after she'd gone. Her mother sometimes said it was Ginny who'd saved her life and Ginny had a feeling this was why she was so tolerant of her further education in the ways of business. Ginny remained fascinated by herbs and had a small room in their beautiful house to grow, dry and mix them. She was sure she could help this vibrant young man who took his pain so philosophically.

'Come to my house,' she suggested. '43 Paradise Street. Over there, in Southwark.'

'Oh I couldn't intrude, miss.'

'You wouldn't be,' Ginny said simply. 'Father welcomes all comers.'

'Virginia! Are you coming, girl?'

Ginny jumped and turned to see her father waiting for her. The sun was starting to dip down over the crowded horizon and it was time to get home and dress for dinner. She could already imagine the fuss her mother would make over her hair when she heard they had an eligible guest coming for dinner. Pushing it impatiently out of her eyes she took a deep breath and hastened to Josiah's side, not allowing herself so much as a glance back at the attractive young lighterman.

On the waterfront, Edward watched Ginny go, his heart racing faster than it would fighting a tricky tidal set. Although she was now being swept up by the riverside crowds, he could still see her pretty, oval face and her wide, compassionate eyes. He looked down at his calloused hands. Would he dare take her up on her offer of healing? She'd seemed very open about it but he wasn't so sure the rest of her family would be.

43 Paradise Street. The address sang round his brain however much he wanted to forget it. He'd find it tomorrow, he told himself, just to satisfy his curiosity. It wouldn't be that hard. He'd been to the waterman's school for several years and had done well. He could read his letters and his numbers and he knew his way around the river like the back of his own hand. Finding Paradise Street would be no problem at all – what he'd do when he got there, however, was much, much tougher.

'Oi! Ned. Move over there, lad, and let me in.'

Edward turned to see his father whipping his boat round on the current to come to rest beside his own. Jumping back onboard he guided his stern out to make space as his younger brother Ralph leapt from his father's boat and tied the heavy ropes up to the docking rings.

'Good day, Ned?'

'The best.'

It was out before Edward could stop it and he turned away as his father peered closely at him. Stephen Allerdice had been a lighterman for forty-odd years and knew as well as any man how hard a trade it was, especially when you were starting out. Unlike young Ralph, who had to work with his father at all times, Edward had his provisional licence and could operate his boat alone. He could not yet, however, command the higher fees of the freeman which meant that the canny merchants were always eager for his services. If he wasn't careful, a young lighterman could spend dawn till dusk on the river – and half the night too. Sure enough, even now a portly merchant was descending on him.

'You there, lighterman! Allerdice.' Edward set his face into a polite smile and tipped his hat to the man. 'I need twelve barrels of rum bringing ashore immediately.'

'Now, sir? But night is falling.' Edward cocked his head

towards the horizon where the sun was bruising across the buildings of the city. 'It's dangerous to run the river at night.'

He gazed with studied innocence at the merchant who sighed and squirmed a purse out from beneath his bulging belly.

'I'll pay double.'

'Done.'

Stephen nodded proudly to his son as he lifted a barrel of his own cargo and headed for the warehouse beyond. Ralph followed with a similar load, but, as Edward negotiated terms, he saw his brother drop his load down to take a stone from the ground and send it spinning carelessly across the swirling river. Once the merchant was gone he seized his arm.

'You don't go playing like that when there's customers about, Ralph. We have to make a living here; we don't do this for fun.'

Stephen, returning for the next barrel, stepped up beside his older son and together they faced the miscreant. Ralph had always been a bit wild and Stephen had bound him to the trade a few months ago in the hope that it would steady him. So far, however, that didn't seem to have happened.

'You can unload the rest of the cargo, Ralph,' he said, his voice steely. 'Perhaps that way you'll learn to do it properly. I'm off home to your mother. Edward, you'll keep an eye on the lad, make sure he does his job properly?'

'I will, Father.'

'Good. We'll make a lighterman of you if it kills us, Ralph Allerdice.'

Ralph stood at Edward's side as their father strode down the rough side street towards home.

'Goody goody!'

'Sorry?'

'You heard me. You think you're so clever with your big boat all of your own don't you? I saw you over there, making eyes at that young lady in all her finery. You want to watch it, our Ned. You're not as grand as you think.'

'No,' Edward snapped back, stung, 'but at least I earn money to keep this family in food, which is more than you do. Now get unloading and I'll be back in half an hour to check up on you.'

'Yes, sir!'

The salute was mocking but Edward had no trouble ignoring it. Harder to disregard were Ralph's comments on Virginia Marcombe. Furious with himself for even caring, Edward leapt into his boat and shoved it crossly out into the now dark waters of the Thames.

Ralph was gone when he made it back to shore with the merchant's precious barrels but the boat was, at least, unloaded. The little terror could work quickly when he wanted to. Ralph had always been an open, fun little lad but he wasn't making the transition to adulthood well and Edward hoped he'd gone straight home tonight instead of out with his dubious set of friends.

He glanced up at the big clock on the side of the docks. He hadn't time to go home and check on his little brother for he was due at his friend Perry's house for dinner and he was already running late. Once he'd unloaded his wares and collected his welcome payment, he hastened up Cook Hill towards the little cottage Perry shared with Sophie, his wife of less than a year. It was growing cold now and he was grateful for the light and warmth that spilled out onto the street when Sophie answered the door.

'I'm late, Soph. I'm sorry.'

'Not at all, Edward. Perfect timing. Come on in and we can

dish up.'

Perry came forward to shake his friend's hand as Sophie went into the kitchen. Perry and Edward had known each other all their lives. They'd played at the edge of the river as youngsters and endured their rough school years together. Now Perry was a waterman, piloting a passenger wherry across the Thames. He'd inherited the boat from his grandfather, as Edward had his. Theirs were professions that ran in the family, and ran with pride and both lads worked hard.

They went through to the kitchen where Sophie was bustling around putting the finishing touches to dinner. Edward's friend had been sweet on Sophie for as long as either of them could remember and he'd been delighted when Perry had finally plucked up the courage to ask for her hand. Now they lived together in this tiny cottage and soon there would be another member of their family, for Sophie was pregnant with their first child and her neat body was starting to bulge at the middle.

'Getting fat, Soph!' Edward teased now as she set a steaming pot on the scrubbed table.

'It's all those cakes,' Sophie agreed.

They all laughed at that. They had about as many cakes around here as Marie Antoinette's peasants. The three of them settled around the little table.

'Good day?' Perry asked.

'Not bad,' Edward said. 'I had Josiah Marcombe on board.'

'Josiah Marcombe hey! Hob-nobbing with the big-wigs now, are you, Ned?'

Edward flushed, thinking instantly of the girl with luminously pretty face, then remembering Ralph's scathing comments about her.

'Not at all. He just wanted to see on board. You know what

he's like.'

'Not as well as you do, clearly.' Edward flushed. 'Just him, was it?'

'No. He had two merchants with him. Funny looking pair. Oh and his, er, daughter. Virginia, was it?'

Perry looked askance at his friend but said nothing. His wife, however, pounced.

'Looks to me as if our Ned has fallen for someone.'

'Rubbish,' Edward said automatically, but Sophie just looked at him, eyebrows raised and, if truth be told, he was desperate to confide in someone.

'All right, so she was kind of pretty. Not just that, though. She's not some parrot girl in fancy clothes. She really knew what she was talking about. I spoke to her about the new docks. She's different, she . . .'

He dried up as Perry shook his head in horror.

'Oh Ned, Virgina Marcombe? She's way above you even in your wildest dreams. What on earth have you got yourself into?'

'Nothing. I've got myself into nothing. I just clapped eyes on her, I said. She was just interesting, that's all.'

Perry and Sophie looked at each other.

'Uh oh!' Perry said.

'He's got it bad,' his wife agreed.

'I have not!' Edward retorted. 'I can admire a lady without it meaning anything, can't I?'

'Of course you can, Ned,' Perry agreed, still smirking, 'of course you can.'

But they both knew it wasn't true.

Chapter Two

In Paradise Street, Josiah Marcombe was pacing the drawing room awaiting the arrival of the intriguing young Nathan Johnson. He hadn't thought much of the lad on first acquaintance but he'd really come to life when he started talking about boats and Josiah liked that. He liked that very much. His wife, Eliza, had been keen that he got to know the fellow – he was some distant cousin of her family – and he'd invited him and his father to his offices just to please her but it might work out very well indeed.

He looked at his family proudly. Eliza was in her chair, looking very pretty, if a little pale. Her health had been a great concern to him since that terrible illness after Charlotte's birth, but Ginny – his dear Ginny – had done so much to make her stronger. Mary, his second daughter, now sixteen, was playing the harpsichord and little Charlotte was battling with her embroidery. Ginny was at her side, trying to help, but, in truth, she was less talented with the needle than her ten-year-old sister and Josiah smiled at her as she tutted in frustration over the fiddly female pursuit.

Ginny didn't persue normal female things – his fault, he knew – but she was pretty, no denying that, and especially so tonight. She had a sort of glow about her. Perhaps it was that deep-red dress? He hadn't seen her in that before. Or had he? For Josiah dresses sort of melded into one after a while. Any way she was pleasing to the eye; young Nathan would have no cause for complaint there, he was sure of that. It was all looking very promising. He knew Ginny was strong enough to run his business, but not everyone was as far-seeing as him and it would be tough for her dealing in such a male world without a husband at her side. If he could find Ginny a strong, imaginative young man, however, Marcombe's would go from strength to strength.

A knock at the main door, across the hall from the elegant drawing room, made him jump to his feet.

'That will be young Nathan Johnson,' he proclaimed, with a knowing look at his wife.

Eliza rose obligingly and was in place to welcome the young man into the family fold when the butler announced him. Josiah bustled forward to join her.

'Nathan! Welcome. Do make yourself at home. We don't stand on formalities here. A drink? Perhaps some port wine, or malmsey?'

Nathan agreed and took a glass. He stood a little awkwardly in the middle of the room, his lean frame exposed in his tight evening clothes, his hipbone jutting towards the piano where Mary was on to her next piece. It was an exciting new passage of Beethoven and it spared the family finding words to welcome the young man.

'Well that's enough of me,' Mary announced, rising as soon as the last chord had died away.

'Oh surely not,' Nathan protested. 'That was divine.'

Mary blushed as prettily as she could for one with a nose nearly as sharp as young Nathan's. Before she could respond to the summons for further entertainment, however, the bell rang for dinner and the family moved through to the dining room.

It was, as far as a distracted Ginny could remember afterwards, a pleasant enough meal. The duck was excellent, as were the apple pastries. The conversation seemed to flow readily enough but her own contributions were trite to say the least. She'd been quite happy discussing Nathan's undoubtedly interesting ideas on the future of shipping until he'd started waxing lyrical about the adaptability of the lighter boat they'd been on today. Then she'd remembered the way her heart had picked up pace when she'd joined eyes with Edward Allerdice and she'd been struck by how blank she felt towards Nathan Johnson in comparison. The thought of being shackled to him for life depressed her into silence.

She finally escaped to her bedroom a little after ten, relieved to be free of company at last. Now she was about to undress when a tap at her door disturbed her. It was Mary, her hair in ribbons and her eyes shining.

'Nathan seemed nice, don't you think?' she said, the minute Ginny let her in. 'Full of ideas.'

'Yes.'

'Shall you marry him?'

'Mary!'

'What? Father's clearly keen on the idea and you're eighteen now you know, lucky thing.'

'Lucky! I'd rather choose my own husband.'

'Choose your own. . . ! Oh Ginny, come on. No one chooses her own husband.'

'No, but Father might listen to a preference.'

'Do you have a preference?'

Mary looked keenly at her older sister and Ginny flushed

again.

'No, of course not. I'm just saying if I did have, he might, what's that?'

Both girls froze, listening to a groan from the next room. Their mother had retired early, complaining of a headache and clearly she was still suffering. Ginny, grateful to escape Mary's questions, rose immediately and went to Eliza's side.

Her mother was wretched, tossing in her sheets and flinging her arms about. Promising to fetch herbs to bring her some relief, Ginny made her way downstairs towards the little room at the back of the kitchen where she kept her medicinal preparations. A light was burning still in the drawing room and Ginny paused a moment behind the half-closed door, to see her father addressing a fading Nathan over a glass or two of best West Indian rum.

'You're a fine young man,' he was telling him. 'You have some interesting ideas. We could use ideas like that at Marcombe's.'

'Are you . . . are you offering me a job, sir?'

'Perhaps. A position, certainly. These things are delicate, boy. Connections must be made carefully, if you know what I mean.'

'I think so.'

Ginny found herself wincing at her father's clumsy attempts at subtlety and turned, eager to escape, but her dress caught a loose nail on the dresser and tugged at it sending her mother's best china rattling like an alarm. Immediately the two men leapt to their feet.

'Ginny. What are you doing still up?'

'I'm sorry, Father. Mother's in pain and I came for lavender.'

'I see.' He turned to Nathan. 'Ginny's quite an expert with the medicines too, you know.'

Nathan nodded stiffly.

'She's a very accomplished young woman.'

He dared to meet her eye and she saw raw hope in it. Not for her, but for the advancement she could offer him. She didn't blame him. Everyone had to make their way in the world somehow, but she didn't want to be his way.

'I must get upstairs,' she murmured, but Nathan was heading for the front door, bobbing and bowing his way out with many compliments to her father, who then turned back to her.

'Sit with me, Gin, whilst I finish my drink, hey?'

Obligingly Ginny took a seat at his side.

'Do you like him, lass? Do you like young Nathan?'

'He seems very bright,' she offered uncertainly.

'But do you like him?'

'In what way, Father?'

'In every way, girl. Come on, there's no need to be coy with me. We're close, aren't we? I've trusted you with more than most females so surely we can talk on this matter?'

'You want me to marry Nathan, Father?'

'It might work very well, yes. Do you have a better idea?' Ginny flushed and looked down at the rich tapestried rug below her feet. 'Virginia?'

'Of course not, Father, though I'm not sure I'm ready yet. There are many, erm, interesting men out there.'

'Like who?'

'I don't know. Like . . . like that young man in the lighter today.'

It was out before she could stop it. Edward Allerdice had been haunting her thoughts all evening and she was longing to talk about him properly.

'Young man? What young man?'

'The lighterman. He seemed very purposeful, don't you think? Polite too. He—'

'The lighterman!' Cut off, Ginny sneaked a peep at her father as he registered what she was saying and was alarmed to see his dear face turn a violent shade of purple. 'The lighterman? Young Allerdice? Now listen here, young lady, no daughter of mine is going to go throwing herself at the lesser orders. Merchants is one thing, but labourers! There are lines, do you hear me? – lines you don't cross! I have compromised myself bringing you up to run my business. Don't think I don't know what they say about me. Don't think I don't know they think I'm mad trusting a mere girl to run Marcombe's. I've put my neck on the line for you, Virginia, and now it's time for you to pay me the same courtesy. You will marry a man who gives strength and standing to your position and that of your family. You will marry a man I choose. Do you understand?'

Ginny ducked her head, heavy with a terrible sense of having disappointed her beloved father.

'Yes, sir.'

'Good. Now get yourself up to your mother and don't let me hear any more of this nonsense. Lighterman indeed!'

Ginny fled, promising herself that she would do as her father had asked and forget Edward Allerdice but already her heart felt heavy with the loss.

Edward strolled home the long way along the river-front and paused to stare across at the tall houses of Southwark, wondering under which distant roof Ginny lay. He knew this was an impossible romance but here, beneath the stars and the iridescent moon he could indulge himself for a moment. It was good to have something to occupy his mind other than ships and cargoes and the endless pull of the tides. Eventually, however, he roused himself and headed for home. He had a big job on tomorrow and would have to be up early. It was time he got himself to bed.

As he approached the Allerdice home, however, it became apparent that all was not well inside. A light was burning in the tiny parlour and raised voices could be heard spilling out onto the narrow street. With a sigh, Edward pushed open the door and went inside.

'You'll bring shame on the Allerdice name, Ralph,' he heard, 'and I've had enough of it.'

Edward rolled his eyes. Clearly Ralph hadn't gone straight home after unloading the boat. Taking a deep breath, he pushed on the parlour door and went in to see what was wrong this time.

His mother sat by the fire in a rocking chair, his sister Molly at her side. Molly glanced over and caught Edward's eye with a rueful grimace. They were the elder and most responsible siblings. They'd got on well all their lives and were both easily irritated by Ralph's careless ways. The boy himself was standing, the picture of contrition, as always, in the middle of the room with their father looming over him.

'You're almost sixteen, Ralph. You're as good as a man and yet you persist in acting like a child. Are you not ashamed of yourself?'

'Yes, sir. Oh I am, sir. It's just that . . .'

'What?'

'Gus dared me.'

Gus was Ralph's new pal and a real rogue. Edward glanced over at Molly for an explanation of what the pair of them had been up to this time.

'They sneaked into the building works at the docks,' she whispered. 'He was trying to steal a foundation stone when he got caught by the night watchman.'

Edward sighed. When was his brother ever going to learn any sense? It wasn't even as if he'd have been able to carry a foundation stone if he'd got his hands on one. He stepped forward.

'Do you not have a mind of your own, Ralph?'

Ralph's cheeks burned as Edward's point found its mark. Stephen turned to his eldest.

'I thought you were going to see him right,' he snapped, his usually placid temper inflamed by an embarrassing visit from the authorities.

'I'm sorry, Father. He'd gone when I got back. I assumed he'd come back here. I'll keep a closer eye in future.'

'I don't need to be babied,' Ralph spat.

'Oh I think you do,' his father said ominously. 'From now on you'll stay at your brother's side whenever you're not on the boat with me. We'll drill some responsibility into you somehow.'

Stephen looked at Edward who nodded obediently.

'I'll try and keep him by me, Father. I'm sure he'll be better in future – won't you, Ralph?'

Ralph glanced at his dark-browed father and gave in with ill grace.

'Yes, Ned.'

'Good. Now off to bed with you. It's late.'

As Ralph scuttled away Edward sank onto the low bench along one side of the room.

'How's young Perry?' his mother asked, anxious to ease the tension.

'He's fine, Mum.'

'And that lovely wife of his?'

Edward sighed. His mother had made it perfectly clear that she'd like to see him similarly paired off.

'Sophie's fine, Mum. Very well. The baby's starting to show

and it seems to suit her.'

'Good. That's good. Nothing settles a man like a wife and child.'

'I'm very settled,' Edward objected, but Maude just shook her head and made for the door, ruffling his hair as she passed.

'You'd make some lucky girl a wonderful husband, Ned dear,' she said quietly and then she was gone.

Edward sat listening to her and Stephen heading up to bed as Molly damped down the fire. He hadn't had much to do with girls to date. He'd been too busy with his apprenticeship. He'd danced with a few at the parties in the Waterman's Hall every Christmas but had never felt anything for any of them, not the way he knew Perry felt about Sophie. Not the way he was sure he could feel about Ginny. He flushed and Molly, noticing, came to sit at his side.

'You've got someone in mind, haven't you?'

'For what?' he asked defensively.

'You know, for marriage.'

'Rubbish. Why would I have?'

'You've got that look about you.'

Edward turned his face away a little. What was this 'look'? Had Cupid scrawled something across his face? First Sophie and now Molly – was he really that obvious?

'All right,' he conceded cautiously, 'I might have seen a girl I like, but that's all.'

'So far.'

'So far.'

Oh, but it was an impossible dream!

'Is she pretty?'

'Very.'

'Good-natured?'

'I think so.'

'Does she like you?'

Edward stood up.

'Heavens, Molly, how should I know?'

'I bet she does.'

'Why?'

'You're a good-looking lad, Ned. Bit of a scruff maybe, but not a bad catch I'd have thought.'

Not a bad catch! Edward grimaced. Josiah Marcombe certainly wouldn't see it that way, but Molly was peering at him again now, a sly smile around her full lips.

'I think I know who it is.'

'You do?'

How could she? He'd only told Perry and Sophie. Surely Cupid hadn't been that obvious?

'It's Lucy, isn't it?'

Edward blinked disbelievingly. Lucy Smith was Molly's best friend. She was often around the house and Edward had an easy, teasing relationship with her. She meant nothing to him but Molly took his hesitation for agreement.

'Oh that is so romantic, Ned! It would just be perfect. My best brother and my best friend. Can I be bridesmaid?'

Edward stared at her in horror.

'Steady on, Mol. There'll be no bridesmaids yet, and no brides either. There's nothing to it so don't you go blabbing.'

'Oh I won't Ned. Honest I won't.' She reached up and kissed him fondly. 'I'll let you get on with your own affairs your own way.'

He laughed. 'That'd be a first.'

'Cheeky.'

'Nosy! Now come on, Mol, let's get up to bed.'

Edward watched as Molly climbed the narrow stairs ahead of him. Why hadn't he disillusioned her? Usually he told Molly everything, but this wasn't usual. He'd been reckless already confiding in Perry and Sophie. If word of how he felt got out, his father would be as mad with him as he'd been with Ralph this evening. Lightermen stuck to their own and didn't go giving themselves airs and reckless ambitions.

He crept into his room and found his slim pallet bed at the foot of the larger one where his two brothers slept together. A shaft of moonlight was shining in through the curtains and in the silvery light he gazed at his rough hands. Let them blister, as they always had. He would have to steer clear of Paradise Street and its beautiful, dangerous inhabitant before he brought trouble on himself and his dear family. Yet, as Edward lay down to try and sleep, he knew already that this woman had stirred his usually cautious soul and that she might, in fact, be worth an awful lot of trouble.

Chapter Three

Edward stood at the entrance to Paradise Street and gulped. A tall lad, he was usually in command wherever he went but here, in the shadow of these grand houses, he felt like a little kid running errands alone for the first time. Somewhere down the wide street was number 43 and inside it, behind one of the shiny front doors, was Virginia Marcombe.

Turn around, Edward's head was saying. *Turn around and go back over London Bridge to your own folk. You don't belong here.* For some reason, though, the message wasn't getting through to his feet.

I'll just walk straight past, he told himself. *No harm in that, is there? Just a quick stroll to see where she lives.*

Before his more sensible side could pipe up again, Edward stepped forward and sneaked a look at the nearest door: number 25. *Keep going, Ned, keep going.* Number 37, number 41, and suddenly there it was: number 43.

It was no different from its neighbours, but to Edward it seemed to leap out immediately. It was a big, square-fronted building with four smart steps up to a burgundy door with a gleaming brass knocker dead centre. Tall bay windows rose up on either side, discreet curtains hiding the lives within from prying eyes such as his. There were blackened railings in front and a narrow passageway to one side. Edward stared down it longingly. It must run to the trade entrance at the back of the house. If only he'd thought to buy a basket of whelks he could legitimately have tried his luck at the kitchen door. As it was . . .

'Hello.'

Edward nearly jumped out of his skin. A girl was sitting on a garden wall on the other side of the railings, legs swinging beneath a lacy frock and a china doll perched at her side. She looked about ten, the same age as his own little sister Mercy, and her inquisitive eyes were trained straight on him.

'Hello,' he managed, trying to smile.

'I'm Charlotte Marcombe and this is Betsy.' The little girl leapt down, waving her doll, and came towards him with her neat hand outstretched. 'Pleased to meet you.'

Reluctantly, Edward put out his own hand and was surprised to have it clasped firmly.

'Are you looking for Cook?' Charlotte asked. 'Because it's her afternoon off. The maids too. There's just me and Martha here'.

She waved a dismissive hand towards a bored-looking maid in the shadow of the house.

'No, I . . . I was looking for your sister.'

'Mary?'

'No. Miss Vir—Virginia.' Heavens, he was stuttering like a fool.

'Oh Ginny! Why d'you want her?'

It was a better question than she realized. Edward felt hot under his Sunday-best collar and ran a nervous finger beneath it.

'She was, er, going to recommend some herbs to me.'

The youngster seemed to find nothing strange in this. She nodded wisely.

'Ginny's always doing stuff with herbs. She saved my mother when I nearly killed her, you know. This way.'

Before Edward could process this startling information Charlotte was off, apparently leading him down the side path and through a wrought iron gate towards Virginia Marcombe. Martha, who clearly had very little control over her young charge, followed meekly, and there was no way Edward could stop himself from doing likewise, though he glanced back fearfully as the world he knew receded and he stepped into what must truly be the Garden of Eden.

Little paths meandered between carefully tended beds all bursting with more lush plantlife than Edward had ever seen outside of Brockley woods. A glance up at the solid brick of the big house and its neighbours confirmed that he was indeed still in London Town but this was a part of it he'd never even known existed.

He turned to the child but she'd gone, sucked into the vegetation. Hearing a voice, he looked uncertainly between two rounded bushes and came face to face not with Charlotte but with Virginia herself. She gasped.

'Oh, I'm so sorry,' Edward said. 'I didn't mean to intrude. I was just passing and your sister—'

'My sister had you by the throat before you could draw breath? She does that.'

To Edward's great relief, Virginia was smiling. He looked round for Charlotte but the child had slipped away, her nursemaid with her, and they were alone. Edward felt almost unbearably alive. He was acutely aware of the rich colours of the midsummer flowers around them, of the hypnotic buzz of the bees and the whisper of the breeze across the tall foliage that shaded them from view of the house. For a moment Ginny just stood there, staring at him, her face as open as if she were a flower herself, and then she said, 'You came for the herbs I promised you?'

It sounded cheap like that.

'Not at all,' Edward said swiftly. 'I wouldn't dream of—'

'I'd be happy to help.'

'I really don't need them. I've been doing this job for years and the blisters always heal sooner or later.'

'Yes, but why suffer if you don't have to?'

That stumped him.

'We live in an age of such progress,' Ginny went on. 'Every day new discoveries are being made. There are men travelling the earth and finding such plants as we could never even dream of.'

'To tell truth,' Edward said, 'your own garden is a revelation to me.'

She blinked and Edward cursed his foolish honesty, but her face held no scorn as she said, 'I'm lucky, I know, but you could be luckier.'

'Sorry?'

'You're a man, Edward. You're free. You could travel if you wanted. You could get out there and roam the world. You're not stuck in London in skirts.'

She said it with such venom that Edward almost laughed out loud.

'You seem to have quite a lot of freedom for . . . erm . . .'

'For a girl. I know. As I said, I'm lucky but it doesn't stop me wanting more. I'm so restricted.'

Edward looked at the fire in her eyes and felt a thrill rush through him. This was a woman who spoke her mind and it emboldened him to do the same.

'Being a girl isn't the only thing that restricts, Miss Marcombe.'

'It's Ginny, please, and what do you mean?'

'Ginny, right. Well, er, Ginny, I mean there are other things that stop a man – or a woman for that matter – from sailing the world. Like money and family and responsibility. If I went off adventuring who would feed my family? My mother and father rely on my wage.'

Virginia stared at him, a flush creeping across her pretty skin.

'You're right. I'm spoilt, aren't I?'

'No! Not spoilt, miss, er, Ginny. Not spoilt at all just . . . privileged?'

'Privileged, yes.' She smiled sheepishly and Edward's vulnerable heart pounded.

Here was a woman he could happily talk to all day, a woman with ideas and dreams beyond the hearth. Her enthusiasm was infectious and sparked Edward's ready imagination. He'd seen a man in the tavern last week talking about something called curry leaves that gave stews a musky, aromatic taste and helped them to last longer in hot weather. He'd mentioned it to his family, but no one had seemed that interested. It didn't do to 'get ideas' in his part of London.

'It's not wrong to have advantages, Ginny,' he said earnestly, 'especially if you use them well. And with our new docks we'll be perfectly placed to see all the changes first hand.'

'Absolutely.' She'd recovered now; her eyes were shining again. 'Last year I persuaded Father to invest in the Africa Association. They're sending men to explore the possibilities of trade in Africa. Exploration is the future, Edward, don't you think? We live in such exciting times and I hope Marcombe's will make the most of it.'

She was moving on through the garden now, but curiosity wriggled in Edward's body, making him bold enough to stop her with more questions.

'How does your business work, Ginny?'

She smiled over her shoulder at him.

'It's simple, really. We buy goods in bulk from abroad then we sell them on at a higher price. You can sell a barrel of rum for two or even three times what you bought it for.'

'Really?' Edward exclaimed. 'But anyone could do that. Sorry. I mean . . . I'm not normally so rude.'

'It's fine. You only speak the truth, Edward. It's called speculating.'

'Speculating.' He tried the word out and liked the way it rolled off his tongue.

Ginny had slowly been wandering along one of the paths that led towards the house and now it opened out onto a neat little courtyard overlooked by the biggest window Edward had ever seen. A door stood slightly ajar and to this she gestured now.

'Come inside, Edward, and I can find you the ointment I promised.'

Edward glanced at the window. He couldn't see anyone but that didn't mean they weren't there. He didn't want to create trouble for Virginia and turned to say as much but she'd already gone in. Not wanting to seem rude, Edward had little choice but to follow and the moment he was inside he was so glad he had.

The room was small and cosy, not dissimilar to his mother's kitchen at home apart from the amazing amount of light flooding in through the vast window. Bunches of herbs and flowers hung to dry from a big rack over the sturdy central table. Along the windowsill stood pots of more delicate plants and on the back wall a big dresser groaned under the weight of numerous tins and jars.

'You do all this?' Edward asked, drawn further into the room.

'Most of it.'

'It's like an apothecary – only prettier.'

Ginny laughed at that and, as he turned, she caught his hand. Edward felt her touch sizzle through him.

'Does it hurt?' she asked, as he jumped.

'No! No, it doesn't hurt.'

She glanced up at him, then down again quickly. Letting his hand drop, she moved to the shelves and selected a pot.

'Witch hazel,' she told him. 'It's very good for sores normally, though yours are, well, unusual.'

'Not where I come from they're not.'

She smiled.

'Well, just think, you could be the first lighterman to be free of blisters.'

'I'd be famous and you'd be rich!'

Realizing the stupidity of this statement, Edward ground to a halt. For a moment they'd connected as two people, but now he was aware again of the contrast in their stations.

'I'd better go. What do I owe you?'

'Nothing. It's my pleasure.'

'But . . .'

'Pay me if it works. You will come and let me know?'

'It'd be my honour.'

Edward moved reluctantly to the door then thought of something else.

'You don't have anything to ease discomfort in pregnancy do you?' he asked.

Perry had been alone at church this morning as poor Sophie had been feeling ill. He looked hopefully at Ginny but her pretty face had closed up a little, as if the sun had ceased to shine on it.

'For your wife?' she asked stiffly.

'My. . . ? Oh no! No, no, no. My friend's wife. Sophie. I've no wife. No.'

'Your friend's wife? '

Ginny gathered herself quickly and Edward suppressed a sudden thrill that his own marital status mattered to her.

'She's about seven months gone, I think,' he said, 'and Perry, that's my friend, said she was laid up in all sorts of discomfort this morning.'

'Did he say where?'

'Her back mainly, I think. I have to confess I didn't really ask for details. It was just seeing all your medicines here, I thought . . .'

'Of course. Here. This is raspberry leaf tea. It's meant to ease the pressure of the babe. And lavender would help her relax. And—'

'You know a lot about it.'

'I studied herbs when my mother had birthing fever after Charlotte. It's an interesting area.'

Edward smiled.

'What?' Ginny objected, squaring her slim shoulders. 'It is!'

'Oh I'm sure,' Edward agreed quickly. 'I was just thinking that at least this explains why Charlotte told me she'd nearly killed her mother.'

Ginny laughed.

'The minx! She loves to shock. Here, let me package some of this up for you.'

Edward stood to one side as she worked, admiring her deft fingers and concentrated movements.

'Do you import medicines?' he asked, suddenly.

'Do I? Oh you mean Marcombe's? Er, no, not really. Food stuffs mainly. Why?'

'I just thought, with what you were saying about the new discoveries and all, that maybe there was a market there. After all, no one likes being ill do they?'

She was staring at him.

'Ginny? Sorry. Stupid idea. Presumptuous too. I'm sure you know what you're doing. I'll just–'

'No, no Edward, it's not that. I think it's a wonderful idea. I don't know why I never thought of it myself. I'll put it to Father.'

'I just thought it might be nice to put both things you love together.'

'It would. Edward, you're . . .'

But what he was to Virginia, Edward would have no chance to find out for at that moment a door banged loudly upstairs and a deep voice called, 'Hello! Where is everyone? Eliza? Virginia? I'm home!'

The young pair in the drying room froze.

'It's my father.'

'I'll go.'

She nodded. Although she had refused to acknowledge Edward's lower status, they both knew Josiah would not be as lenient. Edward moved to the door but a touch on his arm stopped him.

'For your friend's wife.'

Ginny shoved the package into his hands.

'But I must pay you for this. I–'

'Another time. I'm so sorry.'

'I understand.'

Ducking out of the door Edward dived back into the shelter of the plants. His heart was beating wildly, as much from the touch of the amazing girl he'd spent the last precious half-hour with as from fear of what her father would do if he found out.

Ginny forced herself to turn away from the tantalizing view of the young lighterman leaving her herb room. Splashing cold water on her flushed cheeks, she raced up the stairs to greet her father feeling as giddy as young Charlotte. Josiah had been collared by her mother and they were heading upstairs to their private rooms, no doubt to discuss another of her little sister's misdemeanours. Or perhaps not, for as they disappeared around the bend in the grand staircase she heard Josiah saying, 'They seem a good family, my dear. Apparently Mr Johnson is related to the Duke of Northumberland.'

Mr Johnson? Nathan! It seemed maybe she, not Charlotte, was the subject of her parent's private discussion today. The thought made Ginny's stomach squirm. Swallowing hard, she dived into the drawing room and made straight for one of the long bay windows just in time to see Edward let himself cautiously out of the side gate and hasten into the street.

'Ginny?' Mary, who had been practising her music when Ginny burst in came to join her sister. 'What are you looking at?'

She too peered down the street.

'Don't you think has a fine figure?' Ginny said, pointing to Edward.

'Who? Him?' Mary wrinkled her nose up. 'Ginny, who is he? Look at his clothes!'

'Never mind his clothes, Mary, look how tall he is, how broad his shoulders, how well he carries himself.'

'How well he . . .' Mary turned to stare in disbelief at her older sister. 'Ginny, what are you thinking of? Who is he? What is he?'

'Mary! His name is Edward Allerdice and he is a human being like you or I.'

'All right, all right, I'm sorry. But how do you know him? What does he do?'

'He's a lighterman.'

Mary looked quizzical. Unlike her sister she had little interest in the mechanics of her father's shipping business. She was a self-contained young woman happiest at her harpsichord or lute.

'A lighterman,' Ginny repeated, leaning over to catch the last glimpse of Edward as he turned on to Tooley Street to head for the river. 'He rows one of the boats that carry cargo from the ships to the shore. It's a very skilled job.'

'I'm sure it is and I'm sure he's very good at it, but what's it to do with us?'

'He rowed Father and me the other day. We got talking. He had these horrendous blisters – you should see them, Mary – and I offered him some ointment to try and help.'

'Ointment?' Mary looked sceptical now. 'You asked him here to our house to give him ointment?'

'Yes. If it works, Mary, it could be big business. There are hundreds of watermen.'

'I see. So this is a business arrangement, is it?'

'Yes.'

'And his broad shoulders help there, do they?'

Ginny flushed and Mary drew her sister away from the window and down onto the curved couch nearby. She glanced anxiously at the door and leaned in to talk in a strained whisper.

'Ginny, don't do this to yourself. You can't have this . . . this lighterman. It's ridiculous.'

Ginny refused to reply.

'You're to marry Nathan Johnson,' Mary pushed on. 'Father wants it, Ginny, and what Father wants—'

'Father gets. I know Mary, but this is my life, not his, and I don't want to marry Nathan.'

'Why ever not?' Mary's voice rose and she took a deep breath before continuing. 'Nathan's a fine young man, Ginny. He comes from a good family. He's full of interesting ideas and he's, well, he's far from poor looking is he?'

Mary had turned raspberry-leaf pink and Ginny looked at her curiously.

'You like him, Mary.'

'I do not.'

'You do. You want him for yourself.'

Mary rose, anger bristling from her usually calm young body.

'So what if I do? So what if I think he's kind and gentle and interesting? What I want is of no consequence. I know that and the sooner you work it out the happier you'll be.'

'But, Mary, if *you* like him . . .'

Mary batted crossly at a rogue tear and Ginny rose too to throw her arms round her sister.

'It's 1800, Mary. Big things are happening. It's permitted to want more, isn't it? Life's changing.'

For a second Mary looked at Ginny as if she might believe her but then she shook her head.

'Not fast enough it isn't,' she retorted, and pulled away as footsteps on the stairs proclaimed their father's heavy descent.

The door flew open and there he was, beaming from ear to ear.

'Mary. Virginia, my dear. And where's little Charlotte?'

The two older girls looked blank but behind them a bright voice called: 'Here Papa!'

Slowly, Ginny and Mary turned and stared in horror as their devious little sister and her dolly popped up from behind the couch on which they'd just a moment before been pouring out the dangerous secrets of their hearts.

Chapter Four

Later that week Edward was still struggling to banish Ginny from his mind. He had hidden her ointment under his bed and taken to applying it last thing at night. It smelled of her magical garden and the brief time he'd spent there and, whilst it didn't seem to be having much effect on his hands, it was setting his mind spinning. As he'd plied his trade these last days he'd found treacherous thoughts arriving uninvited in his head, such as exactly how God decided who ended up on which side of the mighty Thames. And why it was so wrong to try and change.

Revolutionary nonsense, his father's voice said in his head whenever it happened. Everyone had been stunned by the news from France in the last years and no one more so than Stephen Allerdice. As far as Edward's father was concerned, you kept your head down, did your job and looked after your own. It wasn't a bad philosophy, but Edward couldn't help wondering how much you missed if you never turned your eyes beyond your own stretch of the mighty river.

On Wednesday evening, just as the Allerdices were finishing work for the day, a long-awaited ship was spotted sailing up the river. Edward and Stephen glanced at each other. They were both tired but there were men in the warehouses waiting eagerly for this particular cargo and that meant there was money to be made.

'Oh, Father, no!' Ralph cried, catching his father's look. 'We've been at it all day and I want to go training. Please, Ned, take me training.'

Edward groaned. His brother was competing in the much celebrated Doggett's Coat and Badge race in a month's time and was constantly begging for help with his training. The race had been established almost hundred years ago when a Drury Lane comedian had been impressed by a young waterman's skill and bravery in rowing him home late one stormy night. He'd bequeathed six pounds to fund an orange coat and silver badge for the winner of an apprentice waterman's race every year. The race had caught the city's imagination and the winner now had civic and ceremonial duties in the year after his victory.

If Ralph won it could be the making of him and Edward knew he should be pleased that the lad was showing an interest in something other than getting into trouble, but the last thing he wanted to do at the end of a heavy day's work was to go and watch him scull up and down the river. Stephen, however, did not want Ralph out unsupervised, especially with the reckless Gus in tow, so too often that was exactly what Edward had to do. Tonight would be no exception if Ralph had his way but the ship was drawing closer.

'Sorry, Ralph, work to do.'

Ralph's brow furrowed.

'But, Ned, it's a beautiful evening. You surely can't want to spend it humping barrels?'

Beside him, Stephen bristled.

'You're absolutely right, Ralph, the last thing we want to do is hump barrels, but work's work, young man, and money's money.'

'Yes, and those scoundrels with their fancy big ships and their fancy big warehouses make loads out of us.'

'We don't do so badly out of them, Son.'

'Ha!' Ralph kicked at the side of the boat and it wobbled. 'It's slavery, that's what it is.'

'It's a free economy,' Edward put in from his own boat. 'There's money to be made for those prepared to go for it. D'you know that you can sell on a barrel of rum for more than twice the price you buy it in at? Three times if it's scarce.'

'What are you saying, lad?' Stephen's voice was sharp.

'I'm saying that if we could buy some there's a good profit to be made. More than we make here.'

'Are you turning your nose up at our trade, Ned?'

'No, Father! Not at all. I'm just saying that there's opportunities.'

Stephen snorted. 'And where'll you get the money to buy rum, young man? One barrel would cost you a month's wages.'

'I know that, Father. We'd have to club together, form a, well, a company. All put a bit in each and get a lot back out.'

'Gambling,' Stephen muttered.

'Speculating,' Edward corrected, trying not to think of the young woman who'd taught him the word.

'Throwing good money away,' Stephen snapped. 'It's nonsense. Look lively lad, she's dropping anchor. And as for you . . .'

He turned to Ralph but his younger son had gone, slipping away as they were arguing. Stephen cast a frantic eye along the docks but there was no sign of him.

'That boy is going to be in so much trouble!' Stephen rumbled, thoroughly riled now, but with merchants on the shore with money to spend there was no time to go chasing after him.

Edward watched as Stephen gritted his teeth and set off to the ship, then followed respectfully in his wake, reminding himself to keep his 'revolutionary' ideas quiet in future.

It must have been over two long, hard hours later when the cry went up along the bank:

'Mr Allerdice. Mr Stephen Allerdice!'

Stephen and Edward coming in to dock, their arms weary and their bellies gnawingly empty, heard the cry and glanced at each other fearfully. Manoeuvring skilfully in to land they leapt out.

'Stephen.'

It was Silas Walker, a long-standing friend of Stephen's dead father and head of the Council of Watermen.

'Silas?'

'It's your lad, Stephen.'

'Ralph? What's he done now?' Stephen turned as two other lightermen, big and burly with faces like a winter storm, marched up the docks with Ralph firmly in their grasp. 'Ralph! What's going on?'

A crowd had gathered to see what was up and Edward felt his cheeks flush as he faced his brother.

'Racing, wasn't he? Him and that other lad – Gus Richardson – rascals. Right down the trading stream, as if we were all out on a jolly. Some of us have work to do, Stephen, you should know that, and we don't need reckless, jumped-up little whippersnappers like your Ralph here disregarding us. About had me over he did. Rammed straight into me. No sorry. Wouldn't even have stopped if I hadn't got him by the scruff. It's not good enough, Stephen. You're a fine man and your father, God rest his soul, was a fine man too, but this—' he shook Ralph onto the ground in front of him—'this is a disgrace to the name Allerdice.'

Edward closed his eyes briefly as Ralph grovelled on the dirty ground before Stephen. His father was as stiff as an oar, his back rigid with shame.

'I'm very sorry for anyone who's been disrupted and you can rest assured this reckless behaviour will not go unpunished.'

'Too right,' one of the offended men spat. 'It's Waterman's Hall for you.'

Stephen glanced at Silas who nodded sadly.

"Fraid so, Stephen. First thing tomorrow. Private hearing,' he added more loudly to the assembled crowd. 'Now off with you all. It's late and the tide's rising. I think we've all had enough for one night.'

Edward sighed, took a step forward and hauled his younger brother to his feet. Stephen, he was sure, would not have had enough. It had been a tough night and, thanks to Ralph, it wasn't over yet.

The next morning saw the three men on the steps of the Waterman's Hall, a beautiful modern building in the imposing classical style. This was where Edward had come two years ago to be accepted into the Company of Watermen. That had been a happy day, the whole family in their best clothes, his mother tearily delighted and his father with his chest puffed out in pride at passing the family trade down the line. Edward glanced across at Stephen now and saw shame written all through the taut lines of his trim lighterman's body.

At forty-five, Stephen had a good few years of work in him yet but last night's bitter recriminations seemed to have aged him ten years. Edward turned to frown on Ralph, the cause of all this distress. The boy had the grace to look cowed and, to be fair, his eyes were red with a night's weeping. Stephen hadn't thrashed his son but the stinging blows he'd dealt with his tongue wouldn't heal quickly, Edward was sure.

The big door opened and Silas stood there.

'You may come in now.'

Taking a deep breath, Edward tucked a quiet hand under his father's elbow. Stephen glanced at him, briefly grateful, then set his face again as the Allerdices went in to face the council.

It was blessedly brief but the grim stares of the eight men appointed to govern behaviour on the Thames would stay with Edward for a long time. The punishment – a fine that might have bought half a barrel of rum – would hurt for a while too. The whole family would go without as a result of Ralph's reckless behaviour and it was a bitter morning for them all.

'I'm sorry, Father,' Ralph tried, when they were released into an incongruously sunny morning.

'As you should be,' Stephen grunted, eyes locked onto the great river before them as he stepped away from his crumpled son.

The Thames was alive with action as people crossed to the city on the wherries, dodging the lighters as they moved cargo ashore. Behind the scene the new docks were rising up like a skeleton waiting to be fleshed out and Edward felt a shiver run down his spine at the sight. What if this skeleton was the death knell to his family's future?

'Tough times, Son,' Stephen said.

'Interesting times, Father,' Edward replied staunchly.

'Still keen on becoming a trader hey? Being a lighterman not good enough for you either, Ned?'

Edward heard the hurt in his dear father's voice and turned towards him keenly.

'Not at all, Father, not at all. I love my job and I'm very proud of it.'

The latter, at least, was true, and he heard Stephen draw in a deep breath of relief.

'I know, Ned, and I'm grateful and now I need to ask something more of you.'

'Yes, Father?'

'I need you to keep young Ralph even closer. He looks down enough for now, but the wretched child is like an empty barrel; he'll bob up again before long. I just don't know what I've done wrong there.'

'You've done nothing wrong, Father. Ralph's just, well, Ralph.'

'Hmph!' Stephen turned towards the family's boats. 'I suppose we should be grateful we're still allowed to work. They won't be so lenient next time. Keep an eye on him, Ned, hey, when he's off the boat? For me.'

Edward nodded.

'I will, Father.'

Fleetingly his mind flew to Virginia. How would he ever see her with Ralph in tow?

You shouldn't be seeing her anyway, he told himself sternly and set his broad shoulders to his fate.

That evening Edward arrived at Perry's house with his younger brother in tow. He'd dropped Sophie's herbs off on Sunday and his friend had accosted him earlier that day, looking delighted with their effect.

'Sophie's drunk gallons of that tea, Ned,' he'd told him, 'and we're sleeping with lavender under the pillow. Nice it is, though I smell like a girl in the morning. The lads are full of it.'

He'd grimaced but Edward knew he didn't care. Perry was a family man through and through and it would do Ralph good to see how life could be when you weren't obsessed with looking good for the lads.

'Boring,' Ralph had muttered, when Edward had told him where they were going, but as they all snuggled into Perry's little sitting room and Sophie served up rare mugs of light ale he didn't look too fed up. Indeed, he seemed fascinated by Sophie's belly and when she sank down next to him, he could barely take his eyes off it.

'I feel so much better, Ned, thank you,' Sophie was saying. 'My back aches much less and I've slept so well. I feel wonderful. Where did you get those magical herbs?'

Edward shifted uncomfortably.

'Just from someone I know.'

'Someone you . . .' Sophie's eyes narrowed but then she gave a little cry. 'Ooh!'

'What's up?'

Ralph jumped sideways as Sophie flinched. She looked across at him and grinned.

'Nothing much, just the babe kicking out. It often gets lively in the evenings.'

'Kicking out? Really?' Ralph's eyes went as wide as full moons.

Sophie nodded.

'There it is again. Would you like to feel?'

'Feel?'

'Here.'

She reached for his hand which he surrendered willingly and let fall onto her bulging stomach, fingers spread to feel the mysterious babe.

'There,' Sophie said, 'Did you feel it?'

Ralph's eyes widened.

'I did, I did. Oh, and there again. Have you felt it, Ned?'

Edward shook his head.

'Oh you should. Here, try! You don't mind, do you, Sophie?'

'Not at all.'

Edward wasn't sure he wanted to feel Sophie's baby, but he was grateful for the distraction from the tricky subject of the herbs and pleased to see Ralph so interested. Perhaps it was time to think about finding him a sweetheart? A good woman often kept a man on the straight and narrow, or so the older watermen were always saying. Edward thought of Ginny and felt a sudden rush of fury. If he were his baby sister Mercy he'd fling himself to the floor and scream 'not fair'. Why should some other man get Ginny just because he was born with a big house and shiny doorknocker and enough money to buy crates of rum?

'All right, Ned?'

Sophie's soft voice spoke into his childish thoughts and he shook them off. He was a lucky man with a fine trade, a loving family and a great future ahead of him.

'Just thinking it's time Ralph here got himself a girl,' he said.

Perry laughed.

'And he's not the only one, Ned. Get a move on, mate. Marriage is wonderful, isn't it, Soph?'

'Wonderful,' she agreed, blowing her husband a kiss. 'If,' she added astutely, 'you find the right person to share it with.'

Edward rolled his eyes but was spared having to answer by a sudden pounding of feet up the rough street and a loud banging on the door. Perry leapt up to let Edward's sister Molly in, panting for breath and Edward shot to her side as Lucy Smith panted in behind, wild-eyed and tearful.

'What is it, Mol?' Edward demanded, fear shooting through him. 'Is it Father?'

Stephen had looked tired and drawn when they'd parted

the end of the working day. Had he taken ill? But no, Molly was shaking her head.

'There's a fire,' she panted, 'down at the warehouses. It's bad, Ned. They need all the help they can get. Can you come?'

'Of course.'

'And quick.' It was Lucy who spoke now, her eyes bright with fear. 'My father's in there.'

It wasn't far to the river and Edward, Perry and Ralph joined the throng of watermen running from their homes at the all too familiar cry of 'Fire'. The blaze was lighting up the whole area as it wrapped its vicious tentacles around one of the older, flimsier warehouses. These were the dying buildings that would be largely replaced by the more modern dockland warehouses, but for now they were still a vital part of the river community. The firemen were there and were managing to contain the blaze to the one building but it was a struggle.

'Father!'

Edward heard Lucy's wail behind him and it tugged at his heart. Frank Smith was one of his father's close friends, a big-hearted man who'd always been popular in the community. A nasty accident with an out of control ferry two years ago had cost him a leg and his livelihood on the lighters, but he'd found work in the warehouses which was presumably why he was now trapped inside. Edward ran up to one of the firemen.

'There's a man inside.'

'So I'm told but what can we do, lad? It's red-hot. He'll be a goner by now, I'm afraid.'

Edward looked desperately up at the building. Most of the blaze was in the west side.

'What if he's over there?' he demanded.

'Dunno. He might be all right, but not for long unless we get shifting. Find a bucket or something if you want to help.'

Edward turned away crossly. Men were forming a chain to move water up to throw on the blaze but Edward could already see that was going to take too long for Frank Smith. Calling Perry and Ralph to follow he dived into the alleyway at the side of the warehouse making for the rear where the hoses wouldn't reach.

The heat was intense, even some yards away from the actual flames, and the three young men cowered. A large section of the back wall had crumbled away and they could see that the west part of the warehouse was still sectioned off by a wall of coffee barrels that were burning, but slowly. There was smoke everywhere. Tearing off his shirt Edward wrapped it around his mouth and moved closer.

'Frank? Frank, are you there?'

His voice was muffled so he lifted the shirt to call again and choked badly. It was worth it though.

'Help,' came a thin reply. 'Oh please help. I'm trapped.'

'There!' Perry called from behind Edward.

Following his friend's outstretched finger Edward saw a movement inside, an arm perhaps.

'I'll get him.'

'Ned, no!' Ralph sounded really frightened now. 'You'll die.'

'And so will Frank if we don't do something. Stay here and keep watch. Shout if it looks like the wall's going to go.'

Pointing to the smouldering barrels he took a deep breath of the relatively clear air outside and ran into the building. Frank was calling still and Edward was beside him in five short steps. The older man's one good leg was caught beneath a fallen beam, the far end of which was smouldering sickeningly. Edward dived to try and lift it, feeling sweat break out all over his body at the weight. He was young and strong but it was a big old ship mast and it resisted him.

The heat stung at his eyes and tore at his skin as he strained but then suddenly Perry was beside him, his own shirt tied like Edward's so that only his eyes were visible. The two men shared a brief look then bent to the wood and together managed to shift it enough for Frank to pull himself free. The barrels were burning more wildly now and the heat was intense. They had to get out

'I can't walk, I'm sorry I . . .'

But lifting Frank Smith was nothing after the beam. Edward pulled him into his arms and he and Perry ran for the welcome cool of the night. Ralph was calling frantically and as they stepped outside, one of the lower coffee barrels disintegrated and, a great pile of them fell, spewing flames across the space where the three men had been just seconds before.

'Let's get out of here.'

Edward ducked back down the alleyway and out to the front. Most of the men were so engrossed in fighting the fire that they didn't notice them until Lucy flung herself at Edward screeching, 'Father! Oh, Father, you're alive. Thank God!' Then suddenly everyone was looking as Edward lowered a desperately grateful Frank to the ground.

'He'll need a doctor,' Edward said, then sank down himself, feeling suddenly weak as if all the fear he'd ignored inside the flaming warehouse had just caught up with him.

'Well done, mate.'

Perry sat beside him and the two men clasped each other briefly.

'You, too, though you were mad to come in with me. What would Soph do without you?'

'She won't have to, Ned. I'll never leave her.'

Edward nodded but then suddenly the two men were mobbed as the rest of Lucy's family descended, falling on Edward with tearful thanks and praise for his bravery. Edward tried to brush it away, but before he could stop them they were lifting both him and Perry up on their shoulders and carrying them down the docks like heroes.

Despite his embarrassment Edward felt warmed by the simple display of love. These were his people. This was his world and he had earned his place in it. He found himself staring down at Lucy, running at his side with her prettily open face turned up to his and willing himself to see in her eyes something, anything, of the spark he had from Virginia Marcombe. But there was nothing.

Edward felt frustration blaze like the now dying flames of the warehouse behind them. Life would be so much simpler if he could just fall for Lucy Smith, but how could he when he was already way off the edge – an unwelcome visitor in Paradise? As a doctor arrived to take Frank for treatment, Edward fought his way back down to earth. He needed to be rescued himself somehow, for he had a nasty feeling that if he persisted with this irresistible liaison he was going to get more badly burned than Lucy's father could ever have been.

Chapter Five

'Edward Allerdice, look at you!'

Molly whistled loudly as Edward stepped self-consciously into the little room where his family and friends were gathered after Sunday lunch.

'Very handsome,' Sophie agreed. 'Don't you think, Lucy?'

Lucy Smith quite clearly thought so. Her eyes were wide, the lashes fluttering up at Edward as he stood in the outfit the Sun Fire Office had provided him with just yesterday.

'Don't be ridiculous,' Edward said. 'I look stupid.'

He brushed at the smart blue jacket emblazoned with the distinctive sun badge of his new employers and wished he'd never agreed to his sister's pleas to try it on. Still, he'd have to get used to it as he'd be expected to wear these clothes most of the time now.

Following his bravery in rescuing Frank Smith from the warehouse fire the previous week Edward had been approached by a representative of the Sun Fire Office to join their band of men. In the last fifty years more and more people had been taking out insurance against fire and the company needed strong young men available to be called out at a moment's notice. Anyone insured was given a large, bronze badge to display on the front of their property and in the event of a fire the relevant company would arrive as soon as possible to put it out.

It was a tough business. Firemen arriving at an uninsured property, or one covered by another firm, were instructed to leave it to burn, but insurance wasn't cheap and it was only the rich who could afford to get their homes and businesses covered. Even then, it was hit and miss as fire spread quickly in the old, timber-framed buildings and often the best the firemen could do was to prevent the blaze from spreading elsewhere.

Being a fireman was a risky job but it paid well and many watermen supplemented their basic income in this way. Edward had been uncertain about signing up at first but the chance to improve both his finances and his skills had been too strong to resist. Surely Josiah Marcombe would object less to a fireman than a mere lighterman?

Edward shook his head against his own foolishness. Who was he kidding? Josiah Marcombe would never consider him good enough for his daughter, however many fires he fought. Frank Smith, however, most certainly would.

Lucy had been around the Allerdices' house an awful lot recently, ostensibly to see Molly but no one was fooled. Edward's mother was delighted and she and Molly were forever 'accidentally' leaving the pair of them alone. Lucy had made her feelings quite clear, but Edward could find no way of reciprocating them and it was becoming horribly awkward.

'When do you start?' she asked him now, rising to admire his silver badge and getting a little closer to him than was necessary.

'Tomorrow, officially, but it all depends when a fire breaks out. It could be days or it could be weeks.'

'But you know what to do, Edward?'

'Sort of. The training was fairly basic.'

That was putting it mildly. Edward and two other new

recruits had been with a senior officer for little more than an hour yesterday, mainly learning how to operate the pumps on the fire-engine.

'Good though, I bet.' Perry leaned forward eagerly.

'Very,' Edward agreed. 'I have to admit, I enjoyed it. You should see the engine they have. It's an ingenious contraption, like a big water-tank on wheels with all these foottreadles and pulling levers that let us squirt the water at the flames so fast.'

Edward's eyes glowed. He'd been fascinated by the machine and keen to learn all he could. After the daily monotony of paddling his boat, it had been a welcome stimulation.

'It sounds amazing,' Perry said now. 'And all that extra money, too. Just think, Soph, what that would buy for the babe.'

Sophie placed a soft hand on her husband's knee.

'It wouldn't buy it a father, my love.'

Perry looked down and Edward smiled sympathetically at his friend. Perry had been keen to join Edward in offering his services, but Sophie had begged him not to.

'Sophie's right, Perry,' he said now. 'It's a dangerous business for a man with a family to support.'

'Not that I think you're going to get in trouble or anything, Edward,' Sophie said hastily.

'Just me,' Perry said glumly at her side.

She turned and kissed him.

'You should be glad you're so precious to me.'

He looked into her eyes and smiled at last.

'I am, Soph. I am. And I don't want to miss out on any time with you or the baby. You're the most important things in the world to me. It's just a bit, well, frustrating.'

Edward went over and clapped him on the back.

'Tell you what, why don't you let me try it out for a month

or two and if I'm still whole at the end maybe Sophie will think again?'

'Maybe,' Sophie agreed, not sounding very convinced.

Perry grinned. 'Looks like you're the guinea-pig then. Tough being single, hey?'

Lucy let out a little squeak.

'I wouldn't mind my husband being a fireman, especially not if he was as strong and brave as you are, Edward.'

'Quite,' his mother agreed crisply. 'You wouldn't want to let it stop you settling down, my boy.'

Edward tried to smile, though in truth he'd rather face any blaze than this trial-by-family.

'I think I'll go and change again now,' he said quickly, and made his escape.

When he sidled back down the stairs he was relieved to see Perry and Ralph waiting for him.

'Fancy a walk?'

'Love one.'

The three young men stepped out in the street together. It was a warm day and many others were out enjoying the sunshine. Automatically they turned left and headed towards the river, grateful when the street widened out enough to let them walk side by side. Ralph wandered over to the river-bank, gazing long-ingly at the water. With just over a month to his big race, he'd love to go out in his scull but such pursuits were forbidden on the Lord's Day.

'Lucy's keen on you, you know,' Perry said once the younger lad was out of earshot.

'I know, my friend. I'm not stupid.'

'She's a nice girl.'

'She is.'

'But?'

'Oh I don't know. I just don't, well . . . love her.'

Perry laughed at his friend's reluctance to speak the word out loud.

'That might come.'

'It won't.'

'How do you know?'

Edward flushed and looked out across the river. On the opposite bank he could make out the roofline of Paradise Road. Would Ginny be there now? Tending her herbs perhaps? Or eating a rich dinner with her rich family?

'I don't,' he said, but he'd been too slow.

'It's this girl, isn't it? The Marcombe heir?'

Put like that it sounded even more stupid. Edward turned to his friend.

'Maybe. Look, Perry, I know I can't have her, but I also know what I felt when we were together and I don't feel that with Lucy Smith. We'll only end up making each other miserable.'

'Not everyone gets to marry for love, Ned.'

'You did!'

Perry stepped back a little at the ferocity of his friend's words.

'I did,' he agreed softly, then added, 'I took her across the other day, you know.'

'Ginny?'

'Miss Marcombe, yes. I take her and her family quite often. They're on my regular route.'

'Really?' Edward sneaked a look at his friend before fixing his eyes on the eddying Thames. 'So you might be able to, say, pass her a note – just one about the ointment she gave me, of course?'

'Of course. I might. If you really think it's a good idea.'

'It's a terrible idea, Perry, but I would like it. I'd really like it.'
He turned suddenly and grabbed his fellow waterman's arm.
'Imagine, what it would have been like if you'd met Sophie and
everyone had said you couldn't have her? Do you love her for her
money? No! For her station? No! Did it stop you being together?
No! So why does it have to stop me?'

Perry put his hands up.

'I'm not sure, Ned, but it's a brave man who'll risk it.'

'And I'm brave. You saw my uniform!'

He winked at Perry who groaned but nodded.

'Get me the note and I'll do my best, but don't blame me if it
all goes wrong – and don't tell Sophie!'

'Don't tell Sophie what?'

Ralph had popped up again. Perry turned to him smoothly.

'Don't tell her how much I'd love to be a fireman. We don't
want her giving birth early, do we?'

Ralph shook his head, looking more serious than usual.

'It's amazing, isn't it,' he said, 'that she's got a babe inside her?
A real, live person. It's sort of a miracle.'

'It is,' Perry agreed, placing a light arm round the younger
man's shoulders. 'It is a miracle, Ralph, and I won't do anything
to jeopardize my chances of seeing it come to be. Come on now, I
think that's young Lucy heading for home so Ned here is safe to
go back.'

And with a smile, he led the two Allerdice brothers home.

Chapter Six

'Miss Marcombe, how kind of you to join us. Do let me get you a chair.'

Nathan Johnson was up in a flash, ushering Ginny forward into her own father's office and fetching one of the gilt-trimmed chairs for her to sit in. Ginny felt herself flush with indignation at being treated like a guest in her own company, but a quick glance at her father confirmed it would be best not to react.

'Thank you, Mr Johnson,' she said, as politely as she could manage, and satisfied herself with tugging the chair just a little closer to her father's side of the huge desk in a token gesture of defiance. Josiah smiled at her.

'Let's have some refreshments, shall we?'

'Oh that's not necessary, Father. We can just get on with business.'

But Josiah wasn't listening. Clearly intent on turning this meeting into a social occasion he'd rung the bell to summon his secretary and was already ordering port wine and sweet biscuits. Ginny glanced at Nathan.

'Are you well, Miss Marcombe?' he asked eagerly. 'Not that you don't look well. You do. Lovely in fact. I was just . . .'

'I'm very well, thank you, Mr Johnson,' Ginny interrupted, wanting to spare them both the misery of his clumsy addresses.

Nathan was a sweet, earnest young man but there was no spark to him. Ginny found herself thinking of the way Edward Allerdice had spoken to her – so open and honest as if he was simply sharing his thoughts with her rather than trying to impress or coerce. But then, poor Nathan did have her father breathing down his neck so she supposed she ought to be kind to him.

'Nathan is here to show us the new boat designs he was talking about,' Josiah said, leaning across the desk towards the young man.

Ginny watched the easy way he talked to him and felt shut out. Was this how it would be when – if – she was married to him? All these years she'd thought her father genuinely valued her commitment to the company but what if he'd simply been making the best of her until he could get what he really wanted: a man to take over? Ginny shivered. She had no doubt that Nathan would, at best, tolerate a wife's involvement in his work. She'd be shipped off to the nursery as soon as he was tactfully able to manage it and that wasn't how Ginny wanted her future to be. Not at all!

Standing, she went round to her father's shoulder to look at the plans, at the same time aligning herself firmly with Marcombe's. Nathan didn't miss the point but didn't make an issue of it either.

'Here,' he said, pushing the big drawings politely her way. 'Do you see these new boats? So much slimmer and lighter, perfect for the new docks. The way we land goods is going to be transformed and with these boats Marcombe's could be the first to really exploit that. You'd be in the forefront of docking techniques.'

Ginny looked closely at the pictures in front of her. The ships were, indeed, sleek looking vessels with apparently light and manoeuvrable sidings to allow easy passage of goods onto the wharfside. She listened as her father's secretary poured wine and Nathan talked with great enthusiasm about different designs. He certainly seemed to know his subject and you couldn't fault his enthusiasm. There was just one problem.

'How would they work with the lighters?' she asked, when Nathan paused for breath at last.

'Once the docks are built, we won't need lighters,' he said. 'Think how much money that will save!'

Josiah nodded keenly but all Ginny could think about was Edward and the family who relied on his wage. Didn't these two know that they were gleefully contemplating the loss of livelihood for the hundreds of watermen living just across the river from themselves? Didn't they care? And, besides, they were wrong.

'The docks won't accommodate all shipping,' she said. 'Not for many years. There will have to be vast expansion before lighters won't be needed at all and we'd be very foolish indeed to cut off our options.'

'She's right, you know,' Josiah said. 'Knows the trade well, does my daughter.'

Nathan backtracked furiously.

'Of course, sir, she's quite right.' Nathan smiled at Virginia, though it was a little tight. 'But these boats will still be able to accommodate the barges in much the same way as the old ones.'

His words were sure but his tone less so. Josiah picked up on it at once.

'Perhaps we ought to get someone experienced to take a look at these plans of yours. I don't want to be made to look a fool, Nathan.'

'Of course not, sir.' Poor Nathan had gone an unattractive

shade of violet now. He gulped at his wine. 'Perhaps you know someone whose opinion you trust?'

'I do,' Ginny blurted out. Both men looked at her and she controlled her voice. 'That young lighterman who rowed us the other day. Allerdice, was it? He was a very competent boatman, wasn't he, Father?'

Josiah looked straight at his daughter. He noted the spot of colour in her classically pale skin and the gleam in her beautiful eyes.

'Very,' he agreed, 'but too young for our purposes. I'll get old Silas Walker in. He knows everything there is to know about the trade and he'll be discreet too.'

Ginny dropped her head to hide her disappointment. It had been over a week since she'd given Edward the ointment and she'd been hoping he might have had chance to seek her out but, he hadn't come. For a second she thought she'd found a way of legitimately summoning him but now her canny father had snatched it away. Silas Walker might know his trade but he was stooped and thin-faced and warty and a meeting with him had far less appeal than one with Edward Allerdice.

'But enough of business,' Josiah said now. 'What are you doing this evening, Nathan? I've tickets to the theatre for the family, but my youngest isn't really up to it so there's one free if you'd like to join us?'

Ginny gritted her teeth as Nathan accepted eagerly. At least Mary would be pleased.

As Ginny was lacing her sister into her favourite dress for the evening's entertainment, Edward crept away from his family's noisy game of cards and hid up in his bedroom with the precious ink and paper his father bought for keeping the family's accounts. All day long he'd been thinking about what he might say to Ginny, but now that the time had come to write it down he couldn't remember any of his ideas. He'd be lucky if she could even read it. He'd learned his letters at the watermen's school and they were good enough for his scant use, but there was no way they'd match up to the fancy calligraphy of a gentleman. Edward sighed and picked up the pen.

Dear Miss Marcombe, he wrote laboriously.

It was his best script but no doubt her little sister Charlotte could do better already. What next?

Thank you for the ointment which is helping my hands no end.

This was partly true. They were bleeding as much as ever but they worked all the better for the feel of her. Edward reached for the little pot under his pillow, closed his eyes and breathed in the scent of Ginny's lovely herb room. For a moment it was perfect and then, like an axe into his dreams, his imagination heard the sound of the door above and Josiah's confident voice and saw the fear in her face. This was madness. He should crumple up the paper now and throw it away and yet, somehow, he couldn't bring himself to do so. This wasn't about her father: it was about her.

I would like to thank you in person, he wrote quickly, too quickly.

It looked awful. Forcing himself to slow down he continued.

I will be walking in Brockley woods this Sunday afternoon if you should chance to have a moment free. I will be under the old oak if you, and any of your family, are passing. Yours . . . He stopped. Should he sign his name? It would look odd if he didn't and yet, if this note did not find its intended recipient, there could be hell to pay. His poor father had seen the family name dragged through the mud enough by Ralph without Edward adding to his pains.

In the end he put a cowardly *E.A.* and folded the note

carefully before sealing it with unmarked wax. He turned it over and on the front he wrote with care: Virginia Marcombe. A clatter of footsteps made him jump and he shoved the precious note under his pillow with Ginny's ointment just before young Nick burst in.

'What are you doing up here, Ned? It's nearly dark.'

'I'm a bit tired. Thought I'd get an early night.'

'In your clothes?'

'As I said, I'm a bit tired.'

His younger brother looked at him, grimaced, and then, thankfully, left him to it. Ned sank back on the pillow and pulled the note out. Madness or not, he was going to send this – or, rather Perry was – and next Sunday he'd be in the woods to meet whatever fate decreed he deserved.

'Did you enjoy the play, my dear?' Josiah asked Ginny the next day as they stepped onto the passenger wherry to head home from the offices together.

'Oh yes, Father. It was very entertaining.'

'Thought it was tripe myself, but then I'm not an artistic man. Your tastes are so much more refined than mine.'

'Hardly, Father. I'm a businesswoman at heart.'

'Yes, yes, but a woman nonetheless. You're better at all that frilly stuff – parties and theatres and afternoon teas.'

'I can't do afternoon tea, Father. I'm always at work with you.'

'For now, yes.'

Ginny swallowed.

'Father, when I . . . that is, if I . . .'

'What is it, girl? Spit it out.'

'If I were to marry would you not see me continuing at Marcombe's?'

Josiah looked at her. 'Would you want to?'

'Yes!'

'But what about babies?'

'Father! You've brought me up on shipping and accounts books. You can't expect me to forget all that just for babies.'

Behind her Ginny heard a chuckle. She whipped round and stared at the waterman, but he was rowing hard against a tricky bit of tidal current and showed no signs of listening in. Perhaps she was just being suspicious?

'I'm sure you'd be able to come to some arrangement with your husband,' Josiah said.

Ginny thought of snooty-nosed Nathan and doubted it.

'Father, I'd run mad stuck in the house all day. You do know that, don't you? You will take it into account if . . . when . . .'

Josiah put an arm around his daughter's shoulders.

'If that's what you want, my Ginny, that's what I will strive to sort out. You know I only want the best for you.'

Ginny nodded. 'I know, Father. I'd just like to make sure you know what I think that is.'

She felt Josiah tense a little and worried she'd gone too far, but they were reaching the plying place now and had to part to steady themselves as the little boat docked. Ginny stood back to let her father alight first, taking a moment to watch his proud but now slightly stooping back as he stepped on to land. He was very dear to her, as were all her family, but she had to make her own life now and she didn't want it ruined from the outset by the wrong husband.

'Miss?'

Ginny looked up startled. The waterman was waiting to hand her on to shore. Above them her father had met an acquaintance and was moving away with him. Ginny shook off her morbid thoughts and stepped forward, but, as the waterman offered a hand to help her out, she saw that it held a rough piece of paper.

'What. . . ?'

His eyes were a little wild as he glanced from her to her father and thrust the note forward. Feeling her own heart start to pound Ginny took it and shoved it deep into the pocket of her overdress as she stepped on to land.

'Thank you.'

'Pleasure, ma'am.'

With a tip of his cap the man pushed his boat back out onto the water, clearly keen to get away. What had Ginny accepted here? She watched him go. He was a young man with kindly eyes and a quiet manner. He didn't seem dangerous. Clutching the note tight in her left hand Ginny waved to her father, still deep in conversation, and headed for home.

Safely back, she rushed into her herb garden, heading for the bottom corner behind the lavender bushes. Glancing around her she took the note out of her pocket and broke the simple seal. Her eyes moved straight to the bottom where the wobbly letters *E.A.* confirmed the secret hope that had been building inside her since the young waterman had handed it over. It was from Edward.

Sinking on to a little stone bench, Ginny read the note, scarcely even noticing the childishness of the hand for its precious content. He liked the ointment. He wanted to thank her. This Sunday. She felt her heart pick up pace at the mere thought of seeing him again. Ridiculous, really. What had she just told her father? She was a businesswoman, not given to silly female hopes and joys, yet here she was getting all girlish over a simple note.

'Ginny? What's that you've got there, Ginny?'

Ginny jumped and sprang back as Charlotte popped up, bright little eyes narrowed suspiciously. Ever since she'd over-heard Mary and Ginny's conversation she'd taken to following both her older sisters around. Ginny summoned her iciest dignity.

'It's an order for a rheumatism preparation,' she said. 'A new recipe. Quite exciting actually.'

She was rewarded by a grimace of disgust from Charlotte.

'Boring! Come on, Betty, let's go and play.'

Grabbing her doll, the little girl darted off and Ginny breathed again, but for how long? She noted that Edward had offered to see 'any of your family', but she knew as well as he surely had that if this meeting were to take place it would have to be in secret. Could she manage that, she asked herself, and was it a risk worth taking? Yet already she knew such questions were irrelevant – Edward wanted to see her again and she would do everything she could to make sure that happened.

Chapter Seven

Sunday was a glorious day – the sun was shining, a soft breeze was playing through the trees and Brockley woods were bursting with flowers and birdsong. Edward, however, could get little pleasure from it. He'd been dawdling beneath the old oak for almost an hour now but there had been no sign of Virginia.

He'd seen several families enjoying the freshness of the country woods a mile or so out of the bustle of the urban river-side. He'd seen a gang of young lads, hair wild and sticks in their hands, and a painful number of trysting couples, too wrapped up in each other to appreciate the beauty of more than their own private magic. Every time he heard a voice he'd look around hopefully but so far he'd been disappointed. He reminded himself that it must be harder for her to get away than for him and took another strained stroll around the huge tree.

He'd left Ralph with Perry to help construct a cradle. He'd thought his brother would kick up a fuss at this intrusion of work into his one free day but Ralph had agreed meekly enough and even seemed quietly enthusiastic. Indeed, when they'd arrived at his friend's house, he'd rushed inside, chattering away to Sophie about the size of her bump and admiring the work that had already been done on the neat little crib. Edward had stood to one side watching him and thought with pleasure that his little brother might finally be growing up.

Good job, too, a voice had nagged in his head, *if you're going to be irresponsible.* He'd shaken it off and waved his goodbyes, trying to ignore Perry's wink and Sophie's curious eye. He'd been excited then but now he was beginning to feel like more and more of a fool – and a lonely one at that. Perhaps he should go home and accept that this was never going to be.

He took a few steps towards the path back out of the woods and at that moment he saw her walking towards him. She had a light hood over her chestnut curls but still he'd know her anywhere from the way she lit up his world.

'Ginny!' He rushed up and took her hand before he was even aware of his own presumption. 'Oh, I'm sorry, I . . .'

He tried to move back, but she gripped his fingers with her own and he was silenced. They stood there, linked by their fingertips as the birds sang around them.

'This is going to be complicated you know,' Ginny said, in the soft voice he'd heard in his dreams all week.

'Too complicated?' he asked.

'Let's walk.'

She dropped his hand and slotted hers through his arm instead. Together they moved into the woods, automatically taking the darkest, most private path. Edward felt his heart swell as he looked down at her delicate fingers on his arm and knew a surge of protective joy.

'What are you thinking?' Ginny asked.

'Nothing. Well, stupid stuff.'

She laughed.

'Like what? Come on, Edward, talk to me.'

'Like how much I like having you at my side, like how . . . manly it makes me feel. Told you it was stupid.'

She laughed again. It was a wonderful sound.

'How does 'manly' feel?'

'What?'

'I don't know. I'm a mere woman, remember?'

Now it was Edward's turn to laugh.

'There's nothing mere about you, Virginia, and I imagine you know exactly what manly feels like. You run a business after all.'

'Do you mind that?'

'Mind it?' He frowned. 'In what way, mind?'

'It's not very feminine, is it?'

'Oh, Ginny, now who's being stupid. All women run businesses surely? What else is a household? My mother is busy day in day out checking the stock of food for the family, balancing the budget, timing the day, not to mention managing the rest of us. As far as I can see the only difference with what you do is that you get paid for it.'

Ginny stopped dead beneath the trees and Edward stumbled. He turned to her slowly.

'I'm sorry, I've offended you. I didn't mean to belittle Marcombe's. I'm sure there's much more to it than—'

'Edward, sssh! You haven't offended me at all. Quite the opposite. Do you always speak so frankly?'

'I suppose so. Do you not?'

'It's all pretence and flattery in my world. I get bored with it.'

'So I'm a refreshing change?'

'Perhaps, but not in a silly way. Not like a clown, if that's what you mean. I like that I can talk to you without having to pretend. I like that you share your thoughts without filtering them first. I like the way you see life. I like . . . I like you.'

Edward looked down at her bright face, her big eyes looking

into his, her lips turned up. He felt a rush of yearning to throw his arms around her tiny frame and clasp her to him and it took all of his willpower not to do just that.

'You can, you know,' Ginny said, her eyes sparkling. 'You can kiss me.'

Edward needed no further invitation. He reached out a hand and cupped her soft chin as his head dipped to hers and their lips met. He kissed tentatively at first, unsure of his own way and terrified of scaring her off, but, as her lips responded to his own, they moved together and their embrace tightened. Somewhere far off Edward heard the birds whistling and the leaves rustling above them but louder than all of that was the beat of his heart in time with that of the girl in his arms. When they finally broke apart she looked up at him mischievously, showing no sign of embarrassment or fear.

'My ointment didn't work, did it?' she said, taking his hand from her chin and grimacing ruefully at the blisters.

'I think it worked very well,' he asserted, pulling her closer again, loving the way she curved in against him.

'I'm going to make this happen, you know,' she said fiercely.

'You are?'

'If you want me to?'

All at once she looked so uncertain that Edward loved her more than ever.

'Of course I want you to. I want to be with you, Ginny. I want to be with you forever, but I just can't see how that can happen.'

'Give me time,' she said. 'I'll think of something, I promise.'

'I can give you time,' he agreed, 'all the time it takes.'

Then he kissed her again and time didn't seem to matter to either of them anymore. So lost were they in each other that neither of them noticed the rustle of the bush to their right, or the flash of palest-blue Sunday dress, or even the knock of a china dolly's arm against a tree-trunk as Charlotte Marcombe made it away from her big sister and her elicit beau without either of them even knowing she'd been there.

'Virginia! Virginia where are you?!'

Josiah Marcombe's voice echoed imperiously up the stairs to where Mary was sitting alone, playing hymns on the harpsichord. It wasn't her favourite music but it was the Lord's Day and they felt dutiful. Why she was bothering to be dutiful, mind you, she had no idea. Ginny had sneaked off without a chaperone, all pink-cheeked and primped up to the nines and Charlotte had disappeared too. With their mother resting in bed, Mary had been feeling rather fed up, but something about the tone of her father's voice told her things were about to become a whole lot livelier.

'She's gone out, Father,' she called, running to the door and almost bumping into Josiah as he stormed up the elegant staircase.

'Out! Where, out?'

'I'm not sure.' Mary caught a glimpse of her father's companion and flushed. 'I think maybe she went to visit someone sick.'

Mary was pretty certain her sister was doing no such thing but, however cross she was at being abandoned for the afternoon, she didn't want Ginny in trouble. Josiah's eyes narrowed.

'On the Sabbath?'

'What better day to help others, Father?'

'Hmm. And who with?'

'I think a friend called.' Mary turned back to her harpsichord to hide her blushes at this lie. Josiah tutted.

'Hhmm. Well, did she say when she'd be back?'

'No, Father, but tea will be served in less than half an hour so I'm sure she'll be in for that.'

'Half an hour?' Josiah shuffled his large body impatiently about the room before spinning round to his companion who was hovering in the doorway, sneaking glances at Mary. 'I'm so sorry, Nathan.'

The young man jumped.

'Quite all right, sir. Quite all right. Commendable behaviour, I'm sure. And I can wait.'

'Wait? Right, yes. Good. Wait.'

Josiah took another turn about the room, but it was clear he wasn't content. Waiting did not suit him, Mary knew.

'Why don't you go to your study, Father?' she suggested. 'I believe Martha put the newspaper in there earlier. I can call you when Ginny gets home.'

'Study?' Josiah said longingly. 'Newspaper?'

He looked uncomfortably at Nathan, trying to weigh up duty with pleasure. The young man, however, was quick to respond.

'Please feel free, sir. I shall be quite content here. Perhaps your daughter would play for me?'

He glanced at Mary again and she felt her cheeks deepen from rose-pink to full, wanton scarlet and hated herself for it. What was she doing blushing like a silly young thing and over Virginia's beau too? But how could she help it when, ever since Nathan Johnson had come to dinner, her daydreams had been full of him?

'Capital idea,' Josiah agreed. 'You were playing anyway, weren't you, Mary?'

'I'd be delighted to have an audience, sir.'

Josiah beamed and ducked out of the door. The two young people heard his heavy footsteps plod along the landing to his study, then the door shut and they were alone. Mary found herself praying that Virginia wouldn't come back too soon. She knew she couldn't have Nathan for good but a few minutes would be better than nothing.

'What shall I play?' she asked him, sinking onto the piano stool.

He came and stood beside her, moving with greater confidence without the overbearing Josiah around. Mary had to tip her head back to look up at him as he drew closer and she felt her whole body vibrate with his nearness. Was this what all the girls giggled about in school and on walks? Was this love? Mary had always scorned their silliness but now it was happening to her it didn't feel silly at all.

'I don't mind what you play,' he said in his soft, melodic voice. 'I would listen to simple scales with delight if it was your fingers playing them.'

Mary swallowed the ball of uncontrollable emotion rising in her throat – a ridiculous bundle of excitement and joy and quite hideous nerves. She turned to her harpsichord and let her fingers find the keys, calming a little as she lost herself in the music. But still Nathan stood there and whenever Mary looked up her heart fluttered quite impossibly until she began to think it would be better if Ginny came home and spared her this agony of hope.

'You play so beautifully,' Nathan said as the piece drew to a close.

'I love it,' she said simply. 'Plus, I don't have much else to do.'

'You didn't want to go into business with your father?'

His tone was light, his eyes gentle as they looked into hers, and she found herself answering more frankly than she might usually do.

'Only Virginia is allowed inside the offices. She's Father's—' She stopped short of the word 'favourite'. It was petulant and childish.

'Son?' Nathan suggested.

Mary laughed.

'I suppose so, yes. Poor Father. He did so want a boy but we disappointed him every time.'

'Oh I'm sure you could never be a disappointment, Miss Marcombe.'

'Mary, please.'

'Mary.'

He lingered over her name and Mary felt the room draw in around the two of them but suddenly footsteps echoed up the stairs and Charlotte thundered in. She stopped dead when she saw them and wrinkled up her nose.

'Not you too!'

'Sorry?' Mary sensed trouble in her sister's words. 'Where've you been, Lottie? Look at your dress!'

Charlotte flicked carelessly at the green stains on her pretty frock.

'I've been in Brockley woods with Ginny. And you'll never guess who—.'

But Mary wasn't having this. Stepping quickly forward, and brushing accidentally and quite startlingly against Nathan as she went, she grabbed Charlotte by the shoulders.

'It's tea in ten minutes, young lady, and Mother will have a fit if she sees that dress. Now off you go and change and we can talk later.'

Charlotte opened her mouth to protest, but the tinkle of her mother's bell summoning her maid closed it again and she fled to her own room. Mary breathed a sigh of relief.

'The child runs wild,' she said to Nathan. 'She's forever giving Martha the slip. Maybe she thinks she's a boy too?'

'Which leaves you to be the lady of the household – and very beautifully you do it.'

Mary could find no reply and they stood awkwardly, a few steps apart as the front door opened below and they felt their moments of privacy slip away.

'That will be Ginny,' Mary said uncomfortably.

Nathan stiffened at her older sister's name.

'Mary, I . . .'

But she didn't want to hear what she already knew: that he was here to propose to Virginia and that she would never get to be more than a sister to him.

'I know how it is, Nathan,' she said quietly.

It was all she could do to keep her back straight and her hands from wobbling but the figure now being shown upstairs was not her sister but a messenger.

'Tom?' Nathan stepped towards the nervous-looking lad. 'Is everything all right?'

'It's your father, sir,' Tom said, his accent thick. 'He's been taken ill. Proper ill, sir. He says he don't want a doctor but he don't look good to me, sir, so I thought you should know.'

'Oh the poor man,' Mary gasped. 'You must go to him.'

Nathan nodded but looked fearfully down the corridor to where Josiah's study door was still firmly closed.

'I'll tell Father,' Mary said. 'I'm sure he will send his best wishes – as do we all.'

Nathan stepped forward and clasped her hands.

'You're a good woman, Mary. Thank you.'

'My p-p-pleasure,' she managed to stammer and then he was gone, barely even lifting his hat to Ginny who had appeared looking hot and strangely vacant at the front door.

Mary tried not to be pleased at this and stowed away every last fragment of Nathan's kind words to be dwelt on in the privacy of her bedchamber later that night. She didn't wish Mr Johnson senior ill, not at all, but she did hope he might stay just a little unwell for a few days. She wasn't sure she could be composed enough to accept an engagement between Ginny and Nathan just yet – if ever.

Chapter Eight

Dusk was starting to fall when Edward finally finished work the following Wednesday but he barely noticed. His head had been in the clouds since his miraculous afternoon with Ginny Marcombe. Several times he'd been in danger of bumping into a passing boat and some of the other lads had teased him. Last night he'd heard his parents murmuring away in their bedroom next to his and had caught the ominous words 'growing up' and 'marriage', as well as the even more worrying one, 'Lucy'.

He knew they were waiting for him to declare himself and hated the thought of what they would say when they knew of whom he was really dreaming. He could hear his father now: 'ideas above your station', 'reckless foolishness', 'putting us all at risk with your nonsense' and it was all true. If Josiah Marcombe found out Edward had been kissing his daughter, he would boycott the Allerdice lighters, and he wouldn't be the only one. Edward was playing with fire and he knew it, but, God help him, it felt so wonderful.

'Ah, Ned, lad. Heading for home? Excellent. We can walk together.'

Edward turned to see his father bearing down upon him with a knowing gleam in his eye and quivered. Fortune, however, was smiling on him in the shape – for once – of his younger brother.

'Oh no, Ned,' Ralph begged. 'Come and see me train. Please. It's only a few weeks till the Dogget and Coat and I swear Gus is getting faster than me.'

Edward rolled his eyes in a token protest, slapping Ralph heartily on the back and sending the young man stuttering across the wharf.

'Looks like I'm not coming back just yet, Father. Sorry.'

Stephen grunted.

'Glad to see you're staying out of trouble at least,' he said gruffly to Ralph. Then, 'We'll talk later, Ned.'

Edward nodded half-heartedly, but, as his father moved away and Ralph rushed off to fetch his little wherry, his thoughts turned inexorably back to Virginia.

How sweet she had been in his arms, how soft her lips, how beautiful her eyes as she turned them up to his. When would he see her again and where? This waterside part of town was small and tightly knit and they were both wellknown within it. They'd had no chance to arrange anything on Sunday, for the evensong bells had rung out from All Hallows before they'd realized it was anything like as late, and Ginny had had to flee for home. He could see her now, flying down the path with her skirts gathered up around her shapely ankles like some sort of nymph. He sighed.

'Heavens above, man, you've got it bad!'

Edward spun round.

'Perry. Thank God. And I'm fine, thank you very much.'

'Rubbish. I could hear you sighing from halfway across the water. It's her, isn't it? The Marcombe girl.'

'Virginia,' Edward said in a low voice, hushing his friend. 'And it might be.'

'You met her?'

'I may have done.'

'Oh come on, Ned, I'm your oldest friend. You can trust me. You know I won't tell anyone.'

'Except Sophie.'

'Well, yes, obviously Sophie. She's a part of me.'

It was said matter-of-factly, but it stung at Edward's raw heart. How come Perry had it so easy? How come he had the girl of his dreams in his arms every single night? How was that fair?'

'You're a lucky man, Perry,' he mumbled crossly, turning his head to watch Ralph push his little boat out onto the water.

'I am,' Perry agreed. 'And I'm sorry it's not so easy for you, Ned.'

Edward grunted, then forced himself to take a deep breath.

'I know. Sorry, Perry. I'm glad you've got Soph, really I am, and I love her like a sister. I'm just a bit grumpy tonight; don't listen to me. Hey, look at Ralph!'

He pointed as his younger brother steadied his craft and came forward for a racing start. He pulled back hard on the long oars and the two men on the bank saw the bows lift as the boat skimmed off across the water.

'He's really good,' Perry said.

'He is,' Edward agreed, feeling a rare spark of pride as he watched Ralph disappear upstream. He turned back to Perry, determined to be pleasant. 'How's Sophie? Bearing up?'

'Her back's much better with those herbs you got from . . . well, you know.'

'Yes.'

'But she's getting bigger all the time and the little thing's kicking like a mule now.'

'Going to be a boy then?'

'I don't know about that, Ned. I reckon women can be pretty lively too.' He grinned. 'I don't care anyway. As long as it's healthy and Sophie makes it through.'

His voice wavered a little and Edward placed a warm hand on his arm.

'It'll be fine. Sophie's a strong girl and they say Midwife Jones is one of the most skilled of them all.'

Perry nodded.

'You're right, Ned, of course you are, but sometimes I just get this tremor of fear. Everything's so perfect at the moment; I feel sure something's going to go wrong.'

'Now who's sighing, hey?' Edward slung an arm round Perry's shoulder. 'We must be getting old!'

Perry grimaced ruefully.

'I guess so. How about a drink down The Anchor together tomorrow night, hey – before I'm housebound with the babe?'

'I'd like that,' Edward agreed. 'Here comes Ralph again. Look at him go!'

The light was failing but they could both make out Ralph, arm muscles straining as he threw all his strength into pulling the oars through the rough water of the Thames.

'Goodness, Perry,' Edward said. 'The boy might actually stand a chance of winning this race.'

'He might, and I hope I'll be able to take my wife and child to see it.'

'You will,' Edward said. 'I'm sure you will.'

He nodded at his friend but couldn't stop his own thoughts sliding down a less positive thread: would he ever have a wife, let alone a child and, more to the point, would it be the one woman he now wanted more than anyone else in the world?

*

Edward had little time to ponder the next day, however, as the fire alarm went up in the early evening. He tied his boat hastily to the wharfside and ran full tilt towards the blaze, jostling with other firemen and interested passers-by as he went. There were a number of insurers in the area but Edward saw the distinctive sun badge shining out from the burning wall and knew his first test had come.

The fire was in a large private house, part of an extremely elegant and currently very vulnerable terrace – and it left him no time for philosophizing or daydreaming. He was both scared and exhilarated by the many-tongued beast he was fighting and threw himself into the task, his heart pumping as fast as the water he was soon helping to shoot out of the great engine.

The occupants of the house were, thankfully, all out safely and Edward was aware of the family to one side of him, their anxious eyes lit up in the dancing light of the flames that were trying to consume their world. The father, a stocky businessman, looking curiously vulnerable in a smoking jacket and slippers was pacing around, trying to help and largely getting in the firemen's way. His wife hovered down the street, her arms around three small frightened children as neighbours rushed to help.

It was curious to see the smart folks of Ginny's end of town as exposed and human as the more public-living watermen, but Edward had no time to dwell on that. He had a job to do. His muscles ached already from pumping the heavy pedals of the engine but he couldn't stop. The fire had started in the basement of the tall building. If it was allowed to move upstairs it would gut the whole building, quite possibly taking its neighbours with it. The firemen were slowly but surely getting on top of the flames but they hadn't won yet.

Edward wiped beads of sweat from his brow and threw the smart jacket his family had so admired to the floor. His body felt as aflame as the building.

'Keep it coming, lads, keep it coming. We're getting there!'

The chief officer strode round, nudging the engine forward, managing the men. Edward glanced up and, seeing approval in his eyes, worked harder still until he felt like he would explode with the effort. At last, the cry went up: 'It's out! It's all out!'

Still, Edward didn't dare stop until the man to his left, an experienced firemen of some years, put a hand on his arm and pulled him away gently.

'It's all right, Ned. We've done it. We've saved the house.'

Finally Edward allowed himself to step away from the fire-engine. The chief officer led a team inside to check the damage but the outer walls were all intact and the man of the house was coming round, shaking all their hands heartily and promising beer in the nearby tavern. Edward stretched the pain out of his arms and legs. He thought of himself as a fit man, more than able to cope with a heavy lighter on the tricky Thames, but this was something else and he had to admit, he'd loved it. Was that wrong?

'Satisfying, isn't it?' the older man said to him with a wink and Edward allowed himself to smile at last.

'Very satisfying,' he agreed and later, when the chief officer came over and commended him to his face for a valiant first job, he felt a rush of pride.

'You'll make a fine fireman, young Allerdice,' his superior said, chunking his tankard against Ned's. 'I expect great things of you.'

'You'll get them, sir,' Edward replied promptly.

He was pleased with the night. The pay was very welcome, but worth more to him than the coin was the sense of achievement and the suggestion that he could be more than just a lighterman. He could raise himself. Whether he could raise himself far enough for Josiah Marcombe, however, was another matter and the thought of it turned Edward's still rushing blood cold. He felt tired suddenly, weary in heart and in limb. Draining the last of his beer, he made his excuses and stepped out into the darkening night.

It was only as he walked away down the now deserted road that he realized he was less than two minutes from Paradise Street. He was due to meet Perry in The Anchor, but it was more than he could bear not to take a brief detour when he had such a legitimate excuse to be here. Heart picking up pace again, he turned left and made for number 43.

'Charlotte, you heard what Mother said – it's time for bed.'

'But I don't want to go to bed. *You* don't have to go to bed.'

Ginny sighed and rolled her eyes at Mary.

'I'm an adult, Lottie, and so is Mary. You, however, although you don't seem to realize it, are still a child and you need sleep.'

Charlotte stuck out a petulant bottom lip and made a dive towards the underside of the piano.

'Oh no you don't!'

Ginny caught her arm just in time to stop the little girl squirming herself in where they couldn't reach her. Ginny was fast running out of patience. She'd been snappy and anxious all week, she knew. She couldn't get Edward out of her head and had started looking at her world through new eyes, seeing not the luxury or benefits of her life, but its restrictions and crushing expectations.

She longed to face up to her father and tell him how she felt but she'd been his golden girl for so long she couldn't bring herself to shatter him in that way. Yet if the alternative was a life without Edward – and, worse, a life with Nathan Johnson – what choice did she have? Ginny feared the time had come to be brave and was worried she didn't have it in her.

'Bed, Charlotte!' she ordered sharply, propelling the girl towards the door.

Tears sprang into her little sister's eyes at this unusually rough treatment.

'You can't do this to me,' she said.

'Oh I can.'

'You can't. And if you do I'll tell.'

'Tell? Tell what?' Ginny looked down at Charlotte and saw a terrifying gleam in her bright little eyes. She froze and sensed Mary do the same behind her. 'Tell what, Lottie?'

'Tell who I saw you with in Brockley woods on Sunday.' The child squared her shoulders smugly. 'So, do I have to go to bed now?'

Ginny took a deep breath. Charlotte had seen her with Edward. Had she been watching all the time? Had she seen them kiss? A trickle of ice ran down Ginny's spine, but she forced herself to keep her face calm.

'Of course you have to go to bed, Lottie. It's for your own good.'

'But I'll tell Father. I will, Ginny. You know I will.'

Ginny glanced over at Mary who could only shrug helplessly. Did she know, too? And if so, how long before Josiah found out?

'Come on, Lottie,' she said, her voice gentler now. 'I'll tell you a story, all right?'

'A long one?'

'A very long one.'

And a very long one it was too. Charlotte was good at extracting favours; perhaps it was she who should be running Marcombe's business? When Virginia finally came downstairs again she felt satisfied that she'd kept her younger sister on her side for now, but who knew how long it would last? Charlotte was a minx and now she'd sensed a weakness in her oldest sister she wouldn't hesitate to make the most of it. Ginny was on borrowed time.

'Everything all right?' Mary asked tentatively when she came back into the drawing room.

'Fine,' Ginny said. 'For now.'

She crossed to the long window and peered down into the street, straining forward to try and see the river and, beyond it, Edward's home. The gracious curve of Paradise Street, however, kept that view from her.

'Is it that lighterman who was here the other day?'

Mary's voice was soft behind her. Ginny sighed and felt her sister's arms go round her shoulders. She placed her own hands over Mary's and leaned back, comforted.

'He's like no man I've ever met, Mary. Really. I feel so alive when I'm with him, if you know what I mean?'

'Oh, I know.'

Ginny looked over her shoulder into her sister's face and saw the new light in her eyes.

'You do?'

'It doesn't matter.'

'It's Nathan, isn't it? Oh, Mary, what a mess we've got ourselves into.'

Mary squeezed her more tightly and Ginny sighed.

'We must be able to do something, surely, if we do it together.

I know – I'll tell Father you should marry Nathan. After all, what difference does it make which of us it is?'

'I'm not sure, but it's you he has Nathan intended for, Ginny, and you know it.'

'We'll change his mind. If you think Nathan would agree.'

'I think he might, Gin,' Mary whispered, hardly daring to give voice to her fragile hopes. 'But that doesn't help you.'

'No,' Ginny agreed. 'But then, I'm not sure much will help me, especially now Charlotte's got wind of it.'

She peered helplessly down into the street and there, as if he'd been somehow summoned by her longing, stood Edward. Ginny gasped. He was in the new fireman's outfit he'd told her about and he looked even more handsome than before. His hair was all over the place, his jacket slung over his shoulder, and his face sooty. He couldn't have looked more wildly unsuitable if he'd tried – or more appealing. He looked up and their eyes met. Ginny pressed forward, placing a hand on the window, scarcely feeling Mary step away as her whole being was consumed by the man below.

He stared up at her, then brought his free hand to his lips, kissed it and threw the kiss across the air towards her. Her fingers closed automatically around it and she smiled shyly. Then further down the street a door banged and Edward jumped and began to move away. At the last minute he turned back and their eyes met again, locked together in sorrow and joy.

Was this all the contact they would be able to have? It was hardly a good foundation for marriage, was it? Ginny felt a near-hysterical giggle rise in her throat and leaned her burning forehead against the cool glass as Edward moved towards the river that separated their worlds. She didn't need Mary, hovering concernedly in the background, to tell her that this was madness, but it was all she could do not to run down the elegant staircase and out into the street after the man she loved.

Chapter Nine

Edward's head was spinning as he headed out across London Bridge, his long legs striding out as if they could outrun his whirlwind thoughts. He'd seen her. He'd seen Ginny and he'd even dared to blow her a kiss. What's more, she'd caught it. He'd seen her delicate fingers twitch out towards him from behind the great panes of glass. It had been wonderful to see her, but painful too. She'd looked like an exotic creature in a cage – like the beautiful panther he and Perry had once seen paraded through the streets when the circus came to town – and Edward had a horrible feeling she was just as unobtainable.

He turned to head back along his own side of the river, cheeks burning with anger at this situation in which he found himself. It would be good to see Perry for a proper talk. The only time they seemed to get together now was snatched between the demands of grown-up life. How different it was from the joyous hours they'd spent exploring as children. The difference wasn't bad necessarily, but certainly, life was a whole lot more complicated. He smiled ruefully and turned towards The Anchor.

It seemed very lively in town tonight. He could hear shouting and see people out on the streets up ahead. There seemed to be some confusion, panic even, and Edward instinctively tipped his nose up to smell for fire. Nothing.

A young lad shot out of a side alleyway and straight into him. 'Sorry mister.'

'It's all right, but what's wrong? What are you running from?'

The lad barely paused, shouting his reply as he fled down the street: 'The press gang. The press gang are in town!'

Edward stared after him in horror. He'd heard tell that the much-feared Napoleon was winning battles against the allies in Austria. The navy was apparently gathering forces to keep British waters safe from his ruthless march for power, but Ned hadn't realized things were this desperate.

He looked round wildly as more men started to pour down the street, most of them from out of The Anchor. Everyone was afraid of the press gang on the waterfront. If ever the call went out for more men to man the navy vessels, the docks were the first place the dreaded king's officers came. They knew the watermen and lightermen were fit and strong and used to working on the water. They didn't care that they had businesses to maintain and families they loved. They just wanted their muscle and their sea-legs to help them in their gloryquests. Edward's stomach churned. His friend was inside that tavern waiting for him and he was in danger because of it.

Ignoring the cries of 'fool', he pushed against the flow, heading towards the tavern door where he could see the king's officers, sticks raised, rounding up men as if they were dogs. Women were coming out of the houses all around, nightshirted children clinging to their skirts or rucked up on their hips, pleading with the officers to spare their men, but their pleas fell on deaf ears. Edward looked round for Perry, praying that he had not yet left the relative safety of his home, but then, over the confusion of heads, he saw him.

'Perry!'

He started forward but a rough hand grabbed at him and yanked him sideways.

'You look a fit lad.'

Edward turned and glared at the weasly man whose clammy fingers were wrapped around his arm but before he could say anything his superior had pulled him away.

'Fireman,' he said, nodding at Edward's insignia jacket. 'Leave him be.'

The man spat in frustration but let go of Edward and turned to hunt down other prey. For a second, Edward felt relief course through him – he'd been told his status as a fireman made him exempt from the impress but hadn't thought he'd need it, especially not so soon – but then he remembered his friend and fear jabbed at his heart once more.

He fought through the now thinning crowd, but Perry was stuck at the back of the tavern and even as Edward drew close, he saw one of the king's men grab at his arm. Perry had no fireman's badge to save him. Sophie had been too afraid of losing him to allow him to join and now she would lose him anyway.

'You can't take him,' he told the officer.

'Says who?'

'I do. He's a fireman, like me.'

'Right. So where's his uniform then? Where's his badge?'

'Here.'

Edward thrust his own jacket at Perry, urging him with his eyes to take it – to save himself. Edward might as well go to sea. The only thing really holding him here was forbidden to him anyway, but Perry had Sophie and the imminent babe. The officer who had saved Edward earlier, however, was having none of it.

'That's your jacket and you know it. I'll have you up for

perjury if you're not careful. Now clear off and leave us to do our business.'

'But this man has a babe due. He shouldn't have to serve.'

'And who do you suppose will defend this country if he doesn't, hey? Who do you suppose will stop the French scum crawling all over us? What use will that be to his babe then?'

'Take me,' Edward said, unwilling to give up. 'Take me instead.'

'We'll take you as well – if you insist,' the officer leered.

'No!' Perry said. 'No, Edward. You have to stay. If I can't be here, Sophie will need you.'

'See, your friend's talking sense. Here now.' He took a shilling from his leather purse and thrust it at Perry, pushing it deep into his palm. 'You're mine!'

'No!'

'Edward, there's nothing you can do. Nothing.'

'But I must—'

A light had gone out in Perry's eyes and Edward hated to see it. He remembered what his dear friend had said to him the other night about feeling sure something was about to go wrong and now his prophesy was coming true. The brawl was quieting; the officers had their men. They all stood forlornly, trapped by orders of a king who knew nothing of their lives and saw them only as muscle in his imperial struggle.

'You can do one thing, Ned,' Perry called, as the officers started to muster them for the long march down to the naval docks.

'Anything.'

'Get Sophie for me. I'd like to say goodbye.'

Edward nodded, tears shining in his eyes, then he turned and ran.

He'd never seen Sophie cry before. He'd never seen her anything other than calm and good-humoured and it was only now that he had to watch her falling apart that he realized how much not just Perry but he too had relied on her for stability. They'd made it to the docks just in time to see Perry before he was manhandled on board a huge, naval ship. Sophie pleaded with the officer for Perry's release, falling to her knees with her big belly bulging pitifully but he'd refused to be swayed.

'Birthing's women's work anyway. Be glad your husband's doing something useful and when we've fought off Bonaparte, he'll be back. Now stop snivelling, woman.'

He'd allowed her a few short minutes with her husband and Edward had stood aside, pain tearing him apart at the way they clung to each other. It was Edward in the end, responding to a heartbroken plea from Perry's eyes, who'd had to drag her away.

Now he stood, Sophie sobbing in his arms as his friend was sucked into the mass of reluctant seamen on board the looming ship. Time passed and the dock emptied but still they kept vigil. In the deepest part of the night Edward tried to persuade Sophie to leave but she refused and so they stayed, her sobs giving way to bleak grief for them both as a watery dawn rose and the ship cast off and moved out to the far-off horizon, taking all their certainties with it.

Chapter Ten

'You look tired, Father.'

Josiah Marcombe waved away Ginny's concern and lifted another sheaf of papers from his desk.

'Not tired, Virginia my dear, just slowing up. I fear the old cogs aren't turning as smoothly as they used to.'

Josiah smiled at his daughter, but Ginny thought his skin looked pale and blotchy and his eyes suspiciously bright.

'Perhaps you should go home, Father. Take some rest.'

'Rest!' The sudden bellow made Ginny jump back. 'I can't rest, girl. There's business to be done. D'you think I got where I did by taking rest?'

'No, I . . . I'm sorry.'

'Hmph.' Josiah hunched down over his papers, frowning at them. 'I thought you'd understand, Ginny. I thought you, of all people, knew what Marcombe's needed, but maybe I'm wrong.'

Ginny drew herself up tall.

'Of course you're not wrong, Father. I love Marcombe's as much as you, but things are going well at the moment. The docks are progressing on time, our shares have risen considerably and trade is going well. Look.'

She sifted expertly through Josiah's papers and produced

a sheet of figures she'd written out herself just yesterday. They showed a marked rise in Marcombe's position in the market and Ginny had even translated this into a neat little graph to illustrate the point. Her father took it from her, looked it up and down and then nodded.

'Sorry, Ginny. I'm sorry. You do a wonderful job. I don't know what I'd do without you. Come here.'

He held out a hand and Ginny moved forward to take it, not sure whether to be comforted or further concerned by her bluff father's sudden emotion.

'I worry about you, Ginny. You're a clever girl and a brave one too, but you're a girl all the same and this is a man's world.'

'Father, I don't see what difference—'

'Hush, child. You will. Women aren't made to work full time. It's not your fault but—'

'That's nonsense,' Ginny interrupted, indignation making her unusually forthright.

Edward came into her mind – in truth, he was rarely absent these days – and she remembered what he'd said about his own mother's work.

'Running a home is a full-time job,' she told Josiah. 'You have to plan and manage people and control a budget and—'

'And I'm sure you'll be very good at it.'

Ginny bit back the scream that was rising in her throat.

'Why are you saying this, Father?' she asked, through gritted teeth. 'Why now, after all this time of training me up to run the business, are you suggesting I'm not capable? Do you really believe that? Do you really think I'm not good enough?'

Josiah stroked her hand, though it was all she could do not to snatch it away. She loved her father dearly, but sometimes the control that he had over her drove her mad.

'I don't think that, Ginny, really I don't, but I do think you'd be better equipped to cope in the long run with a husband at your side.'

'Why?'

Josiah rose and moved to the office window. Marcombe's was situated right on the banks of the Thames and from here they could see across to where the skeleton of the new docks was being rapidly fleshed out into a living and breathing port. Ginny loved the sight of its majesty. She loved the progress and the opportunities that it represented, but she hated the thought that, simply because of her sex, she might be excluded from making the most of them. She could feel her heart pounding in her chest as she watched the back of the man who held her fate in his hands. It was more stooped than she remembered and the knobbles of his spine stood out through the light summer shirt.

'Father?' she said tremulously, fearing she'd gone too far.

In reply, however, Josiah simply said, 'I believe Nathan Johnson's father is recovering from his sickness. I have invited Nathan for dinner tomorrow night. We need to discuss the new boats we are commissioning. That and . . . other business.'

He had not turned round, but Ginny could read his determination in the set of his shoulders and she knew exactly which other business he was talking about. *It's not business,* she wanted to shout at him. *It's not a transaction, it's my life,* but she didn't dare, not with him in such a strange mood. She closed her eyes, wondering if she could, perhaps, at least hint at exactly which Marcombe girl had won Nathan's affections, but before she could find the words, or the nerve, to speak out, one of the young lads from the warehouse burst into the room.

'You knock!' Josiah thundered, turning now and glowering at the boy who had dared to interrupt.

The boy cowered, cap in hand.

'Sorry, sir. I'm very sorry, but it's pirates, sir.'

'Pirates? Here?'

Josiah glanced around wildly, his sharp eyes clouded with sudden confusion, but the boy was shaking his head.

'Not here, sir. They wouldn't dare make it into British waters, but out at sea, sir. They're saying they attacked the *Queen Charlotte*, sir. I believe the boat suffered only minor damages, but the cargo is gone, sir. All gone.'

The boys eyes had grown as wide as saucers and his voice risen several pitches as he related the tragedy. Ginny sucked in her breath, waiting for Josiah's reaction. It was not going to be good. Everyone knew about the dangers of pirates in foreign waters. Several of their best friends in the shipping world had suffered similar losses, but to date, largely due to the expensive guard Josiah had always insisted on, Marcombe's had remained immune.

She looked at her father. His previously pale skin had darkened alarmingly and his limbs were twitching as if they wanted to go out and take on the pirates themselves. Ginny glanced down at the optimistic little graph she had sketched out yesterday and shuddered. The messenger boy glanced at her nervously and she nodded him out with a reassuring smile. It wasn't his fault and no doubt his wage packet would suffer as much as their own.

He scuttled away gratefully and Ginny felt the whole building tense, waiting for Josiah Marcombe to speak. When he did, however, it was not the bull's roar she'd been expecting.

'I'm too old for this, Virginia,' he said simply, then he lifted his jacket from the coat rack and stepped past her. 'If anyone needs me – or just wishes to gawp at my misfortune – I'll be in the Dog and Duck.'

Ginny gasped. Josiah liked a drink as much as any man but she had never seen him touch a drop before six in the evening and it was barely gone noon now.

'But, Father . . .'

Her words froze in her mouth as Josiah came close and fixed her with icy eyes.

'I'll be in the Dog and Duck, Virginia, and tomorrow night we will have dinner with Nathan Johnson and you will agree to be his wife. As I've said once already, I'm too old for this. Good day.'

And on that he was gone. Ginny stared after him in mounting despair. Why had he changed so much? Why did he suddenly see her as little more than an asset, like one of Nathan's wretched new boats? For a moment she was tempted to escape the building herself, but Ginny wasn't one to give up that easily.

Instead, pushing her shoulders back and lifting her head high, she moved down the corridor to summon Marcombe's senior accountant. Her father might think that the only way she could save the company was by offering herself at the altar, but he was wrong. Virginia could sort this out herself, and she was going to prove it.

A long, hard afternoon later, Ginny had made good progress. The ship attacked had not, in fact, been their own *Queen Charlotte*, but a shared frigate. Losses would not, therefore, be as catastrophic to Marcombe's and with the insurance policy up to date, much of the cost would be absorbed more easily than she had at first feared. It was still a blow, but one they could certainly survive.

As she came out of the offices alone, Ginny felt drained by the work she had put in and weak from having missed her luncheon. She'd survived the afternoon on adrenalin and indignation but now that that was draining away she was left spent and vulnerable to her own, more personal fears. Ginny knew what it meant when her father's face set as it had when he'd left the office earlier in the day. Josiah was determined that tomorrow evening she would agree to become Nathan Johnson's wife and she feared there was little either she or the timid Nathan could do about it.

Ginny's thoughts turned inevitably to Edward. For a few short hours in the woods two Sundays ago life had seemed so simple, so pure, but now it was muddied and tangled once more. Ginny had been brought up to believe that she could meet as an equal with men. That had been her father's doing, but now he was retracting all the promises he had offered and the only man left in the world who seemed to understand what drove Ginny was Edward Allerdice.

Ginny thrust her head in the air and turned her footsteps towards the docks. The boy who was meant to be chaperoning her, gasped, her father disliked her walking past the rougher elements on her way to the ferry home but she stepped out firmly and he had to follow. Josiah was drowning his sorrows in the Dog and Duck anyway and he thought she wasn't up to running the business! Fired up once again, Ginny turned along the row of huge warehouses and landing stages where the lightermen plied their trade, her eyes eagerly scanning the water for the figure she sought.

She was in luck. Edward was unloading a cargo of sugar just a hundred yards or so ahead of her. Quickening her pace, Ginny moved towards him like a magnet to the north. Once she was nearly upon him, however, she paused, taking a moment to enjoy the sight of his strong young body as he lifted the heavy crates with ease. She thought of Nathan's thin, office-worker's frame and grimaced. There was no comparison to her mind, though she knew her father wouldn't share her preference. Josiah would be unable to see past Edward's rough clothes and lack of status and big, dependent family. How shallow of him. Decisively Ginny turned to her father's boy. 'I must speak to this lighterman on business' she told him, then ducked around a pile of crates on the bank and approached.

'Mr Allerdice?'

He spun round, almost dropping the load he held and she had the joy of seeing his eyes light up at the sight of her.

'Ginny! That is—' he glanced around fearfully—' Miss Marcombe. What can I do for you?'

She giggled, feeling all the pressure of the day slipping off her shoulders. Edward's voice was calm and respectful but the grin he was shooting her spoke a different story. This was the man who had held her against him, who had kissed her lips, who had spoken to her like a fascinating individual not just a bargaining tool. She glanced back but the boy was distracted by a squirming crateload of eels.

'I have to see you,' she murmured.

'Now?'

'As soon as you can.'

'Now then.' Edward glanced across to the next boat. 'Ralph, can you watch the cargo for me a minute? I just have to run an errand for Miss Marcombe here.'

The young man looked over and his eyebrows raised, but he nodded in agreement and, with barely a second glance back, Edward left his boat and headed into a side street. As soon as they were out of sight of the wharf, he took Ginny's slender hand in his big one, but he didn't stop moving until they had turned once again into a small alleyway at the back of a row of houses.

It was a slim passage but neither of them had any problem

being close to the other. With no one about, Edward pulled Ginny in against his chest and kissed her over and over again. She gave way to his embraces, losing herself in the feel of him – in the warmth and security his arms offered so unconditionally.

'Oh, Edward,' she murmured against his lips when he finally drew back a little.

'Ginny, my love, you're trembling.'

She looked down and saw that her body was, indeed, shaking against his.

'It's been a hard day. One of our boats was attacked by pirates.'

'Oh no! What does that mean for—'

'Nothing really. I've sorted it out as far as possible but it doesn't matter, not really. Oh Edward . . .'

'Tell me, Ginny.'

His voice was loving but firm. Ginny looked up into his eyes and nodded.

'Tomorrow night a young man called Nathan Johnson is coming to dinner. He's expected to propose to me and I . . . I'm expected to accept. Father has made it perfectly clear. Edward – what are we going to do?'

Edward looked down at the girl in his arms, emotions swirling within him in crazy patterns. 'What are we going to do?' she'd said; 'we,' as if they were a team, a partnership. Elation shot through him at the thought of it, but it barely had a chance to fizz in his heated bloodstream before the reality of what she was saying hit home. Ginny's father wanted her to marry this Nathan fellow and he was, therefore, doomed – as if he'd ever had any hope in the first place anyway! And yet, she'd said 'we', hadn't she, and said it like she meant it?

'We could . . .' Edward hesitated. Did he dare say it? Would she hate him for it? Would she think it was cowardly? And yet what option did they have? He took a deep breath. 'We could run away.'

He looked down at her fearfully but Ginny simply took his words on board and considered them, much as she might a business proposition. He loved the way she cocked her head on one side as she thought. He loved that she hadn't become over-wrought as many girls might. He loved that his hands were round her waist and his lungs were, for this brief moment, sharing the same air as hers.

'Where would we go?' Ginny asked, and now it was Edward's turn to consider.

'We could go to America.'

'We could.'

For a moment there was hope between them. The possibility of going away together, of starting a new life, just them, without all the trammels of social standing, was an exciting one. Just as quickly, though, it died.

'I'd miss Mary,' Ginny admitted. 'And Charlotte. She's grown wild enough as it is, with Mother so poorly. I'm the only one who takes her in hand.'

'Same for me and Ralph,' Edward agreed. 'And my parents would be devastated to lose me. But still . . .'

Ginny shook her head.

'We can't do it, Edward. There are too many others to think of. There must be another way.'

A movement at the far end of the alley caused them to leap apart. A woman came into her tiny yard to shake out a table-cloth. She glanced over and Edward turned his back to shield Ginny from her eyes. Even without glimpsing her face, however, the woman would know that the fabric of Virginia's dress was too rich for these parts and the gossips would be out in force within minutes.

'We have to go,' he said, and she nodded and allowed him to shepherd her back into the street.

'I could just talk to Father,' Ginny said. 'He might listen.'

'He might,' Edward agreed, but they both knew that Josiah condoning a marriage between them was as likely as man learning to fly. Mr Marcombe, shipping magnate, wanted to link his daughter to one of his own, in just the same way as Edward's own parents wished him to make home with Lucy. It was easy. It was fitting. It was the way things were done – but why? Were he and Ginny the only ones to see that people were just people wherever they came from?

It seemed so. Forced to separate as they came into the public eye, the only contact they could maintain was with their eyes – and their hearts. This brief episode had cemented the bond they'd formed in the woods. Theirs had been a courtship with no time for modesty or flirtatious games. It had overwhelmed both of them, but now, almost before it had truly begun, it might be over.

'I just want to be with you,' Edward said, as they headed back towards the wharf and the end of their stolen time together. 'I just want to be with you forever.'

Ginny's young chaperon was darting around searching for her and time was running out. They had taken too many risks already.

'I want that, too,' she said. 'I want us to be like the friends you told me about – the ferryman and his wife. What are their names? Perry and . . .'

Edward stopped and Ginny looked at him puzzled.

'Sophie,' Edward said. 'Her name's Sophie but they're not together anymore.'

'What? But . . .'

'Perry was press-ganged last week. They took him away to fight Napoleon. There was nothing we could do.'

'That's awful.' Ginny's eyes brimmed with instant sorrow. 'Isn't she due to birth soon?'

'In about a month. She's distraught. I know. I had to comfort her as the ship took him away.'

Edward swallowed at the memory of his best friend's wife crumpled in his arms as the babe kicked lustily between them and its father sailed over the horizon. Sophie had been a shadow of herself since Perry had been taken away and there seemed to be nothing anyone could do to console her. Even Ralph, who had gone round to finish off the crib he'd started with Perry, had come home subdued by his time there.

'She looks so sad, Ned,' he'd said. 'It's not right. It's not right at all.'

Edward could only agree, but many things, it seemed, were not right in the world and many people who should be together were kept apart.

'I'm so sorry,' Ginny said at his side.

He nodded.

'We're not the only ones with problems,' he said, daring to use 'we' himself. It sounded so good, even if it was of little use to them. He couldn't see how there could never be a 'we' – an 'Edward and Virginia' – out in the real world, especially not if she was to marry someone else.

'I'll be thinking of you, Ginny,' he said, his voice low as they came out onto the wharf. 'Will you get word to me? Somehow?'

'I will,' she agreed, her voice torn with sorrow, but then, as her boy came panting over, her beautiful head went up and she turned her body square to his and said in a loud, calm voice:

'Thank you Mr, Allerdice. I appreciate your advice. I shall see the new boat plans are adjusted accordingly. Good day.'

She held out a gloved hand for Edward to shake. He did so, his fingers tingling at the final touch of her, and then she was gone, off to catch the ferry that Perry should be rowing. It was all too much for Ned and he had to rub a fierce hand across his eyes before he could return to his work.

'What did a comely lass like that want with the likes of you, Ned?'

Ralph's voice needled and Edward rounded on him. His little brother had been getting a bit above himself lately. He was rowing more and more, mainly against his friend Gus whom he was apparently beating every time they raced. His favourite mantra these days was 'When I win the Doggett'. 'When I win the Doggett I'll have a smarter jacket than your silly fireman's one, Ned.' Or, 'When I win the Doggett all the ladies will want to know me, right, Mol?' Or even 'When I win the Doggett I'll be top dog in this family'. Stephen had soon put paid to that silly boast, but it hadn't stopped Ralph strutting about like a cockerel.

'That's not a "lass",' Edward snapped at him now. 'That's Miss Marcombe, Josiah Marcombe's daughter and she's a lady.'

Ralph wasn't in the slightest bit repressed.

'Bet you wish she weren't,' he chuckled.

Edward wanted to upbraid his cheeky younger brother, but for once he hadn't the heart. After all, what Ralph said was nothing but the truth, and a heartbreaking one at that.

Ginny came home to uproar in the Marcombe household. The maid who answered the door to her looked flustered and teary.

'It's the master, miss. He's taken bad. He's got the sickness and he's got it something rotten.'

'But I only saw him at noon,' Ginny objected.

'It's like that, miss. Takes folks soon as look at them.'

She glanced around fearfully as if this sickness was a beast that might fling its claws around her own neck at any time. Ginny tutted contemptuously and strode inside.

'Take me to him, Martha. I'm sure we'll soon have him better.'

Her confidence, however, failed her a little when she entered her father's grand bedchamber and saw him prostrate on the bed, his skin as pale as earlier but now clammy with fever.

'Father!'

His head twitched but he didn't open his eyes. Mary, however, leapt up from the chair at his side and came rushing across the room.

'Ginny, thank heavens! Where have you been?'

'Working late. What's happened? When did he come home?'

'Two men brought him about an hour ago. Said he'd collapsed in the Dog and Duck. What was he doing in there, Ginny?'

'Pirates,' Ginny replied shortly. 'It's not drastic, but he took it badly.'

'Maybe he's just drunk too much porter?' Mary suggested hopefully.

Ginny laid a hand on their father's forehead and shook her head.

'He's sick, Mary. It was probably already taking hold this morning. He didn't look well then but he refused to rest and now this . . .'

They both looked down at the man who ruled their lives. He looked so fragile in his big bed, his necktie loosened and his greying hair plastered to his head.

'It's just a fever,' Ginny said firmly. 'I shall fetch herbs. Has the doctor been sent for?'

Martha bobbed nervously at their side.

'Yes, ma'am, and he said he'd come as soon as he could but there's a lot of it about.'

She glanced around again.

'Well, go downstairs and wait for him, Martha,' Ginny snapped. 'And bring him up the moment he arrives. Where's Mother?'

'Taken to her bed too,' Mary said. 'I don't think there's much wrong with her but at least she's out of the way.'

The two sisters shared a brief grin but then Mary looked back to their father.

'Will he be all right, Ginny?' she asked.

'I'm sure he will. It's just a fever and he's far from frail.'

Mary nodded, cheered.

'Nathan's father recovered in only a few days,' she offered.

'Did he indeed? And how do you know that, Sis?'

Mary flushed.

'I . . . er . . .'

Ginny put a hand on her arm.

'Don't mind me. You should be glad about this, assuming Father gets better of course. Nathan was meant to be coming to propose to me tomorrow evening.'

'What?'

'Father invited him this morning, but he won't be in a fit state to be entertaining for a while.'

'No,' Mary agreed. 'Thank God for that.' Her glance flew to the sickbed and she added quickly, 'though I'd rather have Father well, obviously.'

'Obviously,' Ginny agreed, going downstairs to find some-thing to ease her father's suffering, 'but at least this gives us a few more days to think of a way out.'

Mary giggled nervously, but as Ginny escaped to her favourite room in the Marcombes' elegant house, her heart was pounding and it was all she could do not to let herself out the back door and run back to the wharf and to Edward.

Chapter Eleven

'Come on, Ned, let's get going, hey?'

Edward looked across to his brother who was champing at the bit to load his last cargo and get back to the wharfside. He didn't blame him. It was a beautiful evening and he knew that with the big race just a week and a half away the lad was dying to get out in his little wherry. That didn't, however, mean he had to rush.

'I've got two more sacks to load, Ralph,' he called. 'You and Father go on ahead.'

The lad needed no urging. Kicking his leg against the side of the boat, he pushed the heavily laden lighter abruptly into the stream, causing Stephen to cry out from his position down in the hold.

'Hold on, Father!' Ralph called gleefully, 'and we'll be back in no time.'

'Don't you rush it, lad,' Stephen's gruff voice said from below. 'Tide's turning and there's some tricky currents out there at the moment.'

'Don't fret, Father,' came the blithe response. 'I know what I'm doing.'

Edward shook his head as Ralph's boat scraped past his own and headed out across the swirling river. The lad was almost dancing on the rowing platform – what on earth had got into him tonight? He glanced round to see if there was a gaggle of girls on the bank he was keen to impress, but he couldn't see anyone. There were just the usual lightermen going about their business.

As he watched Ralph cut out into the stream, however, he noticed another lighter moving in a similar direction and paddled by a similar young man. Gus! They were racing, the little fools, and both with their own fathers obliviously on board.

'Ralph, take care!' he called after his brother. 'Don't do anything—'

But his final word was whipped away on the rising summer breeze. He tried to catch his father's attention to alert him to the danger, but Stephen was climbing up out of the hold and wasn't looking his way.

'Ralph!' Edward bellowed again.

His brother looked over and hesitated and in that moment, Gus's boat pulled ahead. Edward saw Ralph's brow crease and watched in despair as his younger brother turned away from him and put his back behind his long oars. His whole being was focused on beating the boat ahead of him.

They were in the middle of the river now, where the currents eddied back against each other. Usually experienced lightermen zig-zagged their way through them to prevent the clumsy boats from being caught side-on, but tonight both Ralph and Gus were pointing their fathers' crafts straight across the mighty river.

Edward watched in horror, his own cargo forgotten, as Stephen climbed up on to the top deck and realized what was going on. He saw his father go along the narrow walkway towards Ralph, but the young man was fixated on reaching the bank first and didn't seem to be paying any attention to his urgent orders.

Edward barely noticed the giant cargo ship's rope digging into his hand as he clutched on to it for dear life – for Ralph's life. Had the boy no idea what he was risking? The Thames was a tempestuous and merciless mistress and Ralph was teasing her more than she might bear. As Edward watched he forgot the recent sorrow of Perry's departure, he forgot the torment of his snatched meeting with Ginny this afternoon. All he could see was his wild younger brother driving his father and his father's precious boat towards possible destruction.

Yet they were close to the bank now. Perhaps all would be well? Ralph was turning his boat to come into land but Gus was still driving straight forward, keen to sneak a lead. His own father was clinging onto the boat's side rail, yelling at him, but he was paying no more attention than Ralf. They were locked in battle against each other and all around men had stopped to watch. Edward didn't want this race to succeed – the winner, whichever one it was, would be unbearable – but equally he didn't want it to fail.

'Steady, Ralph,' he muttered under his breath. 'Just take it steady.'

He could barely make out his brother's face any longer but he could see his resolve written in every line of his strong young body. He was going to make it. He was even going to win, damn him – but at that moment Gus dug his oar in to make the final turn to land, swinging his lighter round so fast that the heavy cargo shifted inside. The boat wobbled wildly.

Out of the corner of his eye Edward saw Ralph freeze and heard the clunk as the Allerdice lighter rolled into the bank, but his gaze was held by the hideous sight of young Gus's boat as it caught in a vicious eddy and began to tip. He saw fear rip through the lad's body. He saw Gus's father hold out his arms to his son in a desperate plea for . . . what? It was too late. The lighters were big and solid but once they began to go there was no stopping them.

Men ran to the bank as the far edge of the craft dipped below the water level and the vicious Thames rushed in, sucking it under faster than Edward would have imagined possible. Gus's father was helpless before the surge of water. Gus, up high on the rowing deck, flailed for a moment longer, his life suspended for them all to see before he, too, was grabbed by the river and sucked down into its swirling depths. Within seconds the boat and both its crew were gone.

'No!'

Edward heard Ralph's cry echo across the water. It wrenched at his heart. Abandoning the last of his own cargo, he turned his boat back towards the bank, his heart churning as he manoeuvred cautiously across the watery grave. Men were leaping into smaller boats in the vain hope of recovering the lost lightermen. Barrels were bobbing up everywhere, released from the sunken boat, but of either of the two lives there was no sign.

Edward pulled into the bank, tied up his boat and made a run for his family. Ralph was hunched up on the ground, his body, so strong and certain of itself just a short time ago, now crushed and gasping with sorrow. Stephen sat just a heart's space away. He wasn't admonishing Ralph – there was no need for that now – but neither could he bring himself to comfort his reckless son.

Edward dropped to his knees between them and flung an arm round both their shoulders.

'Thank the Lord it wasn't you,' was all he could say.

There'd been enough tragedy recently, and here was more, but not, at least, for them. Edward was spared the job of breaking the awful news to his mother and younger siblings. The Allerdices would all still sleep under the same roof tonight and the frightening escape they'd just had made Edward realize how very precious his family was to him.

He adored Ginny, yes. He had a feeling he would never feel this way about another woman all his life, but, as she'd said herself, there were too many other people to take into account just to run away together like self-indulgent fools. He clasped Stephen and Ralph as the other watermen brought in the barrels, leaving an almost superstitious circle around the sorrowful clutch of Allerdices.

'What have I done, Ned?' Ralph whispered, turning scared eyes to his brother and leaning into his touch as if he were a small child again. 'What the hell have I done?'

Edward just held him tight, much as he'd held Sophie. The lad knew exactly what he'd done and hopefully it would teach him to respect both their mighty mistress, the river Thames, and the fragility of their little lives upon it. As for Edward, he'd learned that making your own way in the world was as complicated and fraught as any trip across the worst water. He still wanted Ginny, wanted her more than anything, but not by some foolhardy shortcut. Somehow, he had to earn Josiah Marcombe's respect and, with it, the right to his daughter's hand in marriage.

'I received a letter.'

Sophie held up a single sheet of paper, already crumpled with much reading. Ralph, sat mournfully on a stool at her feet, glanced at it.

'From Perry?'

'Yes, from Perry. Who else, silly?'

Sophie's smile broadened as she spoke her husband's name

and she clutched the letter to her bulging belly.

'What does he say? Is he well? What's it like in the navy?'

Ralph sat forward, looking interested in something for the first time in over a week. He'd become a shadow of his former boisterous self in the days following Gus Richardson's death. The whole community had turned out for a tearful funeral and Ralph had felt everyone was pointing at him – blaming him. He knew he was already known as a bit of a troublemaker and felt certain that this tragedy had put the seal on the watermen's dislike of him.

He was still working with his father – Stephen would allow nothing else and Ralph longed to please him now – but as soon as he could he escaped the riverside to hide away with his own grief and shame. He'd taken to coming to Sophie's, ostensibly to help her with the lifting and carrying now her time was close, but in reality to absorb some of her soft, non-judgemental calm.

'He says he's fine,' Sophie told him now, reading over the few, spidery lines once again. 'He was never very good at his letters, but he says they're treating him all right and he's not been in any danger yet.' She swallowed the last word hastily and pushed on. 'He says Nelson is a very great man and he's seeing some amazing sights but he'd rather see, see . . .'

She struggled to complete the sentence.

'Soph?' Ralph laid a tentative hand on the girl's knee and she smiled at him, though her eyes were watery. 'He'd rather see his home and his wife any day?' he guessed.

Sophie nodded and snatched a handkerchief out of her pocket to dab away the tears. Ralph patted at her knee, feeling useless.

'He'll be home soon,' he promised.

'I know. Not soon enough though. He thinks he'll be many weeks yet. There's no way he'll be here for . . .'

She nodded down at her belly.

'But back for the Christening no doubt,' Ralph said stoutly.

Sophie sighed and turned her head away.

'He may be, but will I?'

'What?' Ralph leapt up and went round to look at her. 'What did you just say, Sophie? Of course you'll be here.'

'I might not. It's a dangerous business you know, birthing.'

'Not so dangerous these days and Midwife Jones is the best in the business.'

'So everyone keeps saying, but what if she's busy? What if someone else needs her when my time comes? What then?'

'Then you'll do it without her. And, besides, first babies take ages to come. She'll be there I'm sure.'

Sophie looked up at him, startled out of her fear.

'How do you know that, young Ralph?'

He blushed.

'I was asking Mother the other day. I think it's interesting.' He scuffed at the floor with his toe. 'It's wonderful that you have another life inside you, Sophie. Amazing that in, well, not long, there'll be another person in this world. Your baby. I can't wait to see it.'

Sophie grabbed for his hand.

'Me neither, Ralph,' she agreed, smiling now. 'Me neither. Hey, I didn't know you were such a softy?'

He pulled away and sat himself down on the stool abruptly.

'I'm not. I'm a troublemaker. A selfish little troublemaker.'

'Says who?'

'Says everyone down at the docks and they're right. I killed Gus, Sophie, and his father too. I'm a murderer, really.'

Sophie didn't reply for a moment and when she did it was with a soft, gentle voice.

'Is that what *you* think you are?'

'Yes. I think I might join the navy. Start again. If Perry says it's all right then that's good enough for me.'

'Oh Ralph! Don't do that.'

'Why not?'

'We'd miss you. Your family would miss you.'

'Ha!'

'I'd miss you.'

'Really? Why? You'll be all right to lift your own coal again soon enough and besides, Perry will be back.'

Sophie sighed again. 'You're not a murderer, you know, and we don't just like you for the jobs you do. You're lively and bright and fun to be with – well, usually you are – and, besides, haven't you got a race to win?'

Ralph just shrugged and muttered something.

'Ralph?'

He flung his head up defiantly.

'I'm not doing it.'

'Why not?

'Why d'you think?'

'Because of Gus? I see. Do you think he'd have not raced if it had been you in the Thames?'

Ralph's brow creased.

'D'you think he'd have moped around,' Sophie pushed on, 'or d'you think he'd have said "Good – I'll be able to win now that Ralph's out of the way"?'

Her poor attempt at mimicking a man's voice forced a sneaky smile onto Ralph's face but he shook his head still.

'It just doesn't seem right, not after what I did.'

Sophie stood up suddenly, hefting her bulky body out of the chair with surprising speed.

'Now you listen to me, Ralph Allerdice. You did not "do" anything to Gus. He did it to himself. He was racing just as much as you were and all right, so you were both stupid, but just because he paid for it with his life doesn't mean you have to sacrifice yours too. If anything, you owe it to him to live yours even more fully.'

Ralph stared at her, stunned at this burst of eloquence and Sophie shifted from foot to foot.

'Sorry. Probably not my place.'

'No.' Ralph rose to join her. 'No, Soph, you're right. Someone needed to say it. Thanks, I suppose.'

She blushed.

'Not at all. Does that mean you'll race?'

'I don't know. I still think everyone hates me.'

'Rubbish. The Richardsons aren't the first watermen to die, Ralph, and I'm afraid they won't be the last. Tides change. Things move on.'

He still looked uncertain and Sophie placed her hands on her wide hips.

'Now look here,' she said, a twinkle in her eye, 'I've got to birth this baby, so you've got to row in the Doggett's Coat and Badge race.'

'I do?'

'You do and you have to row so hard that the pain almost kills you, because that's what I'll have to do too.' Ralph was smiling now. 'Deal?' Sophie challenged.

'You're a hard woman, Soph but, yes, it's a deal.' He glanced out the little window. 'And as there's still an hour or so's light left in the sky I think I'd better go and practise. If I'm going to do this damn race I want to win it.' He made to move to the door but then hesitated. 'Will you be all right?'

'I'll be fine.'

'I could get Molly to come and be with you.'

She shook her head.

'I think Lucy Smith is going to come and sleep here until the babe comes.'

'Lucy? Edward's Lucy?'

'Hopefully.'

Ralph grinned.

'Well, all right then.' He looked at Sophie then darted forward suddenly and gave her a quick peck on her forehead. 'Thanks again,' he said and then he was gone, renewed energy in his long limbs.

Sophie raised a hand to the spot where his lips had met her skin and smiled. Poor Ralph. He'd had to grow up horribly quickly this week but it seemed that, somehow, he was managing to do so and now, at least, she had the race to look forward to. Taking Perry's letter out of her pocket again, she sank back down into her chair to read his few scruffy but unendingly precious words once more.

Chapter Twelve

'Good job, Edward. You'll make a fine fireman if you carry on like this.'

Ned beamed as he accepted his wage for another successful blaze extinguished before too much damage could be done. It was proving to be a hot summer and people were careless with their cooking fires, preferring to cook outside rather than tend at the hearth. Ned didn't blame them but the number of fires he had now attended had made him very cautious.

Only the other day he'd told his mother off for leaving the griddle cakes cooking whilst she went to the door to chat. She hadn't been best pleased with him and had muttered again about it being time he found a home of his own. Lucy Smith had been around an awful lot recently, turning up her big blue eyes at him and asking him all about his work. She was a lovely girl and would make someone a wonderful wife but she'd drive him mad after a while. He wanted someone with a bit more fire in their belly. He wanted Ginny.

Edward sighed and turned the pennies over in his palm. With his new wages he was saving hard, but it would be a while before he could afford a home of his own and even then, it wouldn't be one he could ever bring Ginny to. She was used to high ceilings and big bay windows and all manner of different rooms and whatever she said about them not mattering to her, Edward knew that in time she would come to resent a lowlier life. Though of course, if they worked together . . .

'Needing more, lad?' the foreman asked into his reverie.

Edward blinked.

'No. Oh no, sir. Thank you.'

'It's just that if you did, there's a nice commission to be made selling our insurance you know. Ten per cent on every new customer you sign up.'

'Really?'

Edward stared at him. He was run off his feet fitting in his work as a lighterman with his fireman duties, but he might be able to find another hour or two if he tried. Who needed sleep anyway?

'How would I do that?' he asked cautiously.

'Simple. Knock on doors. Chat up the ladies of the house. Tell them all about the dangers of fire and what our company can offer. It's not like you'd be cheating them – you've seen what a good service we provide.'

Edward nodded keenly and the foreman turned away to his bag from which he produced several sheets of paper.

'This is the form. It tells them all about what we do and they can sign on the bottom here if they want to join up. You bring that to me with the first month's fee and I give you your cut. Easy.'

Edward took the forms. It did seem easy and, even better, it might give him a good excuse to knock on the Marcombes' front door. He hadn't seen or heard from Ginny at all since the dreaded night that her beau was meant to come calling and he was starting to fear the worst. Had she agreed to the match? Was she severing all contact to try and make it easier for them both?

A tiny voice niggled away inside his head every so often, saying that maybe she was relieved to have been spared the obvious heartache of trying to pursue a relationship with him, but he pushed it away. He hadn't imagined the feeling between them in the alleyway last week and Ginny wasn't a girl to play games. Something else had to have happened and now he might be able to find out what it was.

'Thank you sir.'

'You're welcome, Edward. Good work. We'll make a foreman of you one day.'

Edward bowed his head in pleased acknowledgement. Foreman? Would that be enough for Josiah Marcombe? Probably not. Gripping the forms, Edward turned his steps to Paradise Street before his nerve failed him.

Inside number 43 Ginny looked up from her father's bedside and smiled at her sister.

'How is he?' Mary whispered.

'He's fine, thank you,' said a masculine voice and Josiah raised himself on his pillows and smiled.

'Papa!'

Mary flung herself across the room and into his arms. Josiah, pink-faced and vulnerable in his nightshirt, clutched her to him with uncharacteristic vigour, pulling Ginny close in on his other side as well.

'My girls,' he said. 'I don't know what I've done to deserve you. You and Charlotte, wherever the little minx is.'

'Here, Papa.'

Charlotte leapt out from behind the long window curtains, surprising them all.

'Really, Charlotte,' Ginny remonstrated, 'you must stop

sneaking about.'

The little girl stuck out her bottom lip.

'It's the only way I can find out anything,' she objected. 'You all treat me like a baby.'

Josiah laughed and ruffled her hair.

'You're quite a young lady now, aren't you? You all are and I'm very proud of you.' For a moment Josiah's eyes moistened, then, as if remembering himself, he released his hold on his daughters and shooed them back to a safer distance. 'I shall be up tomorrow, Ginny. You better warn them the boss is coming back in and they can stop slacking.'

Ginny's hackles rose instantly.

'Firstly, Father,' she said coolly, 'you are not well enough to leave the house just yet.'

'I think—'

She put up a hand.

'And, secondly, no one has been slacking. I've made very sure of that.'

Josiah looked at her stiff chin and tight lips and reached, once again, for his eldest daughter's hand.

'I'm sorry, Gin. I'm sure you have. I don't know what Marcombe's would do without you.' He squeezed her hand. 'Can I come in next week if I'm a good boy til then?'

Ginny shook her head but she was smiling now and she returned her father's grip.

'If you're very good,' she said fondly, 'you can come to the Doggett's Coat and Badge race on Saturday. And if you survive that, then you can come back to work.'

'Yes, miss.'

She laughed. 'Good. Now, I'll fetch you some of my thyme and lemon balm tea to perk you up.'

Josiah grunted.

'A glass of ale might do the job just as well,' he suggested hopefully, but Ginny was gone.

She went down the main stairs towards her herb room, but halfway down she became aware of Martha talking to someone at the door.

'Oh no, sir. We can't let you in now, sir. We have the *sickness*!'

Ginny tutted impatiently. Their maid was still insisting on treating the household as if it had the plague, despite Josiah's much improved health and the failure of any of the rest of the family to catch his symptoms. Lifting her skirts, she hurried down the last flight to stop her exaggerations.

'We do not have the sickness, Martha, and . . . oh!'

Ginny barely smothered her gasp of surprise as she saw who was on the doorstep. Edward looked taller and more handsome than ever with his fireman's uniform smartly buttoned up and his hat in his hands. His dark hair was tousled where it had sat and Ginny felt a treacherous longing to pull her hands through it. It was with some effort that she recovered enough composure to address the maid.

'And who is this, Martha?'

'He's a fireman, miss, from some insurance company.'

'Sun,' Edward put in. 'Are you the lady of the house?'

Ginny stifled a giggle.

'I'm her daughter,' she said formally, 'but my mother is indisposed at the moment. Can I help you?'

'I just wondered if you had a moment to talk about fire insurance. It's a rising problem, ma'am, and we can offer very reasonable protection.'

Ginny could see that Edward, too, was having trouble keeping a straight face.

'Well that sounds interesting,' she managed, 'doesn't it, Martha? There was a terrible fire just down the road not many weeks back and Father wouldn't like us to be at risk, if we can avoid it.' She glanced ostentatiously at the clock. 'I think I have a few minutes. Would you like to come in?'

'But, Miss Virginia, the sickness,' Martha hissed.

Ginny just shook her head at the maid and ushered her off to the kitchen where she would doubtless complain to cook about her careless attitude. Ginny didn't care. She showed Edward through into the downstairs parlour, closed the door very carefully and then flung herself into his arms.

'Edward. Oh, my dear Edward, I can't believe you're here.'

She spoke in hushed whispers and he responded, clutching her to him and kissing her between words.

'I *am* selling insurance. Not to you, unless you want it, but to make money. I'm doing well, Ginny. My boss says I might make foreman one day. I could keep you. Not like this of course . . .' He looked around the room.

It was one of the smallest in Ginny's house but was bigger and grander than the main family kitchen at home. He faltered but Ginny wasn't to be put off.

'I'll have money too, Ned. Marcombe's pays quite well you know.'

'I'm sure it does and I'm sure you're very good at it, but—'

'But what?' Ginny stiffened in his arms.

'But will your father let you carry on if you–?'

He stopped short of daring to say 'marry me' but Ginny was kissing him too hard to speak anyway.

'Ginny? Are you all right?'

'Edward Allerdice,' she said. 'I love you.'

The three words echoed round the parlour and they both

stared at each other.

'You do? Why?'

'Why? Because you didn't say I can't work because I'm a woman. Because you didn't say I can't work because I have to have babies. Because you understand me and you don't patronize me and you make me feel so . . . so alive!'

Edward laughed, then clamped his hand over his mouth, aware that Martha might be listening outside.

'I love you too,' he dared to say, loving the sound of the words between them. One thing, though, was bothering him slightly. 'Don't you want to have babies?' he asked nervously.

'Yes! Oh yes, of course I do, Ned. I just don't want that to be *all* I do.'

Edward breathed a sigh of relief.

'Right! No. Why should it be? Mother says that being with small children for too long turns your brains to mush and sends your wits out the back door!'

Now it was Ginny who laughed.

'I should like to meet your mother.'

'I should like you to meet her, too. Oh Ginny . . .' He kissed her again. 'But what about your beau? What about the proposal?'

'Oh that! Father's been ill so it's been put off, but he's getting better now. Nathan's been to call but Father was too ill to see him.'

'So you had to entertain him?' Edward asked, and Ginny thrilled at the spark of jealousy he was unable to keep out of his voice.

'Me and my sister Mary and, believe me, he finds her so much more entertaining.'

'He does? So he might. . . ?'

'Ask for Mary's hand instead? I don't know if he's brave

enough, but they've been together enough this week for me to dare to think he might.'

Hope flared between them, but at that moment a high-pitched voice called 'Ginny! Where are you? Papa wants his tea,' and they jumped away from each other guiltily. With the new space between them came the realization of how very far apart they still were. Edward sighed.

'I will do all I can to make myself worthy of you, Ginny,' he said, a little stiffly now.

'You *are* worthy of me,' she insisted, but before she could say more, the door was flung open and little Charlotte burst in on them.

She looked them up and down suspiciously as Edward scrabbled for his Sun Insurance papers.

'Haven't I met you before?' she demanded.

'Charlotte!' Ginny snapped. 'Where are your manners? Mr Allerdice here is calling to discuss fire insurance with us. Important, do you not think? Or would you rather we left you to burn in your bed – as you deserve.'

Charlotte was not put out. She tossed her long hair and gave Edward another appraising look.

'I like your uniform.'

'Thank you.' Ginny watched, charmed anew as Edward bent down to be on a level with her sister. 'Would you like to try on my hat? My sister Mercy loves wearing it.'

Charlotte accepted the hat and stood on tiptoe to see herself in the mirror over the mantelpiece.

'Is your sister my age?' she asked.

'How old are you?' he countered, adding cleverly, 'I'd say at least eleven.'

Charlotte swelled with pride. 'I'm only ten, but I'm very

grown up for my age.'

Edward grinned. 'You are. That makes my Mercy just a little older than you – though no less inquisitive.'

'Inquisi-what?' Charlotte demanded.

Ginny laughed.

'It means nosy,' she told her bluntly. 'Now, let's show Mr Allerdice out and we can get Papa his tea.'

Reluctantly Charlotte returned the hat to Edward, but she kept herself pinned to his side. Ginny showed him to the door, trying to keep her own desire to do exactly the same in check.

'I shall discuss this with Father,' she said formally as Edward stood on the steps. 'Can I get in touch with you if we decide to go ahead?'

'I could call back,' Edward said. 'Maybe in a few days?'

'Tomorrow?' Charlotte suggested cheekily, before her big sister clamped a controlling hand on her shoulder.

'On Monday perhaps?' Ginny said, trying not to sound too keen. 'Father should be better by then.'

'Once he's been to the race he'll be better,' Charlotte told Edward wisely.

'Race? The Doggett's race? You're going?'

'Of course,' Charlotte said innocently. 'Everyone goes.'

'Indeed,' Edward agreed evenly, 'my brother is racing so I and all my family will be on the bank. Perhaps we'll see you there.'

'I hope so,' Charlotte agreed, but it was Ginny's eye that Edward had caught.

As he turned to walk up the street, her heart squeezed with the joyful knowledge that she would see him again in just a few days. It would be in public, yes, but it would be better than nothing. She closed the door dreamily and made her way to the herb room, Charlotte trotting at her side.

'He's nice,' Charlotte said. Then, 'Is he the one I saw you with in the woods?'

That jolted Ginny out of her dreams.

'Woods? What woods? No. No, you must be mistaken.'

Charlotte just raised one scarily adult eyebrow at her big sister.

'I don't think I am,' she said ominously, before adding, 'really, Gin, you should be nicer to him if you like him.'

Then, with a mischievous grin, she skipped off leaving Ginny's heart beating wildly – though whether more from love or fear she had no way of telling.

Chapter Thirteen

Edward let himself back into his own home with his head spinning. He couldn't believe he'd seen Ginny and, not only that, had had a chance to discuss a possible future together. They'd even talked about babies! He had no idea what he'd done to deserve this woman's regard but he did know that he never, ever wanted to lose it. How on earth they could arrange things so they could make those dreams a reality he had no idea, but for tonight it was enough for him that she so clearly wanted to.

'Ned? Is that you?'

'It's me, Mum.'

'In the kitchen.'

'I'm a bit tired actually. I think I might . . .'

Maud Allerdice appeared in the hallway.

'I've made a cake,' she said, kissing him. 'Come and have a slice.'

'Mum, it's late, I—'

'Apple cake,' she said firmly. 'Your favourite.'

It was clear that this was more of an order than a request and Edward trooped after his mother wondering what she wanted to harangue him about. The same old thing, no doubt. For a brief moment he thought about confiding in her. Whilst Maud took no nonsense, she'd always been a kind and loving mother and she might be able to help.

As he stepped into the kitchen, however, he realized that this was not going to be the time for a quiet chat. The whole family were there. The older members sitting around the big old table whilst Mercy and Nicholas were underneath playing with the house cat, Sugar. His mother's teapot was steaming in the centre and slices of half-eaten apple cake were in front of them all. Ralph was talking, seemingly animated for the first time since Gus's death, and the room was warm and inviting. Edward felt a rush of love for his rough and tumble family and moved forward looking for a seat.

'There's a chair here, Ned!'

Ned froze as Lucy Smith turned and smiled up at him, big eyes as blue as ever beneath hopeful lashes. Why had he not noticed her before?

'Yes,' Molly agreed, turning from the other side of the strategically vacant chair, 'come and sit here, Ned. I'll cut you a slice of cake.'

Lucy, however, had beaten her to it and was fussing over him, pouring tea and cutting cake in a very wifely way. Edward felt his throat constrict and his head begin to pound. Reluctantly he took his seat. 'Something good happened, Ralph?' he forced himself to ask, hoping his younger brother would, at least, divert attention.

For a second Ralph's eyes shadowed, but he shook it off and looked straight at Ned.

'Not good really, but I have decided to race in the Doggett on Saturday.'

Edward looked at the newly lean features of his younger brother and nodded.

'That's good, Ralph. I'm pleased. You've trained so hard for it, it would be a shame to throw it all away now.'

He nodded.

'That's what Sophie said.'

'Sophie? You been round there again, lad? I'll have to tell Perry when he gets back.'

Ralph laughed. 'No danger there. Sophie's a one-man woman. She had a letter today.'

'From Perry? Is he safe?'

'He is. Well, he was when he sent it.'

Again Ralph's brow clouded. His brush with death, albeit it not his own, had tempered his previous reckless optimism.

'And Sophie?' Edward asked quickly. 'Is she well?'

'Very, though she's getting a bit scared about the birth.'

Lucy, who had been hovering closer and closer at Edward's side as he unconsciously leaned away from her towards Ralph, saw her moment and jumped in.

'I'm going to stay with her from tomorrow,' she said, forcing Edward to look her way. 'In case the babe comes in the night and she needs help.'

'That's kind of you, Lucy,' Edward said, meaning it.

The girl blushed furiously.

'I know what it's like to be on your own,' she said in a soft voice, picking at her cake crumbs.

Edward was at a loss.

'So, you'll, er, be good company for each other then,' he offered and heard his mother tut across the table.

Maud rose.

'Well, I think I'd better get these youngsters to bed. Mercy, Nicholas, time to go upstairs please.' There were groans of protest from beneath the table and Maud used them as a good excuse to lever her husband to his feet too. 'You'll help, won't you, Stephen?'

'Of course,' he agreed, looking flustered. 'Come on, children. Leave Sugar alone now.'

With much bustling and protesting, the four of them finally left the room, Maude turning back to say. 'You'll tidy up, won't you, Molly?'

'Oh I'll do it, Mrs A,' Lucy offered. 'It was a wonderful cake – it's the least I can do.'

'Thanks, Luce,' Molly said, also rising. 'Then I can get the hens to bed.'

Edward glanced round him fearfully as the packed room emptied at an alarming rate. Only Ralph remained to protect him from Lucy's attentions. He looked pleadingly at his brother, but now Maud was back again.

'Ralph, sweetie, could you run along to Mrs Franklin for some kindling?'

'Kindling? Now?'

'For the morning, Ralph, or there'll be no breakfast for anyone.'

'But can't I go then?'

'No.'

Ralph looked at his mother, then at the remaining occupants in the kitchen and grinned.

'Oh! Right. I see. Yes, I'll go now.'

'I'll come with you,' Edward offered.

'You will not,' Maud said, adding quickly, 'you've been working very hard all day. The butcher's boy said that fire was a terrible one. You must be worn out. You sit there and rest.'

Edward longed to say that if he was so tired out, bed would be the best place for him but he didn't dare. His mother had engineered him exactly where she wanted him and as far as he could see, there was no way out. He took a nervous sip of his tea as Ralph departed with a mischievous wink.

Lucy rose and bustled around, gathering up plates and cups, clearly working hard to show her figure to its best advantage – and a very nice figure it was too. Lucy was a pretty, open-faced girl with soft, womanly curves and a graceful way of moving. Edward tried hard to imagine what it would be like sharing a home with her. He knew she would be kind and attentive and probably good fun. but all he could see when he looked at her was a sister. He felt none of the jolt of exquisite pain that Ginny sent through him and he knew already that he couldn't live without at least some of that joy. What on earth was he meant to do now?

'So, are you enjoying being a fireman?' Lucy was asking as she poured water from the cast-iron kettle into a bowl to wash the plates.

Edward rose to carry the cups over to her side and she smiled up at him gratefully.

'It's good,' he agreed.

'Is it not very frightening?'

Edward considered.

'A little but we're trained, you know, and it can be quite, well, exciting.'

'Exciting? I suppose so – for a man. I'd be scared stiff!'

She simpered up at him in a way that Edward assumed was meant to make him want to sweep her into his arms and care for her. His thoughts flew to Ginny, so proud and certain of herself. She wouldn't be scared by a fire, he was sure of it. Awkwardly he bundled the cups onto the side. One missed the edge and began to slide and Edward had to dive to catch it before it hit the hard tiles and smashed. The movement threw him against Lucy and she giggled and clutched at him.

'Oh, Ned!'

Edward froze, the cup in one hand and Lucy clinging to the other. She was so very close to him, her face tipped up to his, her lips slightly parted as she held his gaze with her own – and still Edward felt nothing. She was expecting him to say something, he knew, and he hated himself for failing her.

'Lucy, I, er . . .' he began.

He could see hope shimmering in her blue eyes, like sunlight on the Thames, and he had no idea how to tell her that it wasn't going to be – that he couldn't love her as a wife deserved to be loved.

'Yes, Ned?' she prompted coyly when he dried up.

'I know we've seen quite a lot of each other recently,' he tried, 'with you being Molly's friend and all.'

She smiled and leaned even closer so that he could feel her apple-sweet breath against his cheek.

'I don't really come to see Molly,' she confided. 'Well, not just Molly . . .'

Ned suppressed a groan. This was going to be worse than he thought.

'Yes, well, you see, Lucy—'

But at that moment a merciful banging on the door inter-rupted them and a voice called, 'Lucy! Lucy, are you there?'

'It's my little brother,' Lucy gasped, pulling away. 'What can be the matter?'

She darted for the door, Edward behind her, and flung it open. Edward stared gratefully at the person who had saved him from the most embarrassing moment of his life to date, but his happiness soon turned to horror. The young lad was panting on the doorstep, his cheeks flushed and his hair wild from running.

'You have to come,' he said urgently, pointing back up the road. 'It's Sophie, Sophie Miller. She's in pain. It looks like the babe is coming early.'

Chapter Fourteen

'Oh heavens,' Sophie said. 'This is killing me – when is it going to start?'

She strained forward, peering down the river and Lucy, at her side, clutched cautiously at her arm. It was three days now since they'd all believed the baby was on its way and although the contractions had abated and neither Sophie nor the child were showing any signs of distress, everyone around her was concerned. Lucy was not at all sure that Sophie should be out, but she'd refused to miss Ralph's race and she was a hard girl to oppose when her mind was made up. The baby, it seemed, was going to be just the same.

'It'll come when it's ready,' Sophie had said that morning, 'and I'm not going to sit here like some pudding until then. The sun's shining on the river so why waste God's gifts hiding inside?'

She hadn't added that keeping busy was the only thing that stopped her pining for Perry, but Lucy had sensed it and wisely kept quiet, although she was feeling the responsibility of caring for the young mother-to-be. Sophie's own mother would doubt-less have been firmer but she had died many years ago and Lucy could only do her best. Besides, she was keen to go to the race herself.

If it hadn't been for Sophie's untimely contractions the other night she might be betrothed by now. If only Edward wasn't so shy. Lucy knew she was pretty enough. Didn't young Matthew, the fishmonger's boy, always tell her so? He had a soft spot for her, she knew. He was always slipping her an extra bit of halibut or a handful of whelks. He was quite sweet, and funny too, but he wasn't Edward, more's the pity.

Molly kept saying that Ned liked her and teased her by calling her 'sister' but it wasn't Molly who had to get down on one knee. Lucy was beginning to feel just a little foolish with all eyes on her and was desperately hoping that God might shine on her in more ways than one today. She glanced over at Edward but his face was set on the river.

Never mind, she told herself. *He's just worried about his brother. Once the race is over he'll be free to think of . . . of love.*

Her fingers clenched involuntarily at the happy thought and Sophie, around whose arm they were still clutched, squeaked.

'Sorry. Oh, I'm sorry. Are you all right? Are you hurting?'

'Only my arm, silly. You can let go, you know. I'm not going to go tumbling into the river.'

Sheepishly Lucy drew back, taking the chance to sidle closer to Edward. He looked down but his eyes were shaded. Still, it was a very bright day. Lucy smiled up at him.

'Is Ralph nervous?' she asked.

'He was this morning. Up at some ridiculous hour, crashing around and waking us all.'

'It must be very cramped in that bedroom,' she suggested coyly.

'Hmm. Still, I bet he's fine now he's out on the water and can get on with it.'

Edward turned back to the river as the last of the scullers

rowed past them to the start and Lucy suppressed a sigh. *After the race*, she reminded herself. *He'll notice me after the race. For now let him concentrate on Ralph.*

Edward was not, however, concentrating on Ralph at all. His eyes were certainly straining to follow whichever of the now distant watermen was his brother, but his brain was buzzing with thoughts of Ginny. Whenever he dared he scanned the crowd for any sign of her but with half of London lining the bank for the hugely popular race it was hard to see.

The Dogget's Coat and Badge had been popular when it was first started, thanks to the renowned Drury Lane comedian whose inspired idea it had been, but in the hundred years since then it had gained even more momentum. The winner was now recognized as a civic figure with many ceremonial duties in his year of holding the coveted title. The orange coat that was placed on his back at the end of the race was known throughout the City and today was an event that brought rich and poor together in the irresistible glory of sporting triumph.

Edward thought of what winning might mean to Ralph and felt a flicker of envy. Would Josiah Marcombe think more of Edward if he had an orange coat on his back? It was too late now – the race was for initiate watermen only – but it didn't stop Edward feeling the pang of an opportunity lost. A fireman's coat was smart, yes, but it didn't carry the prestige that his younger brother might secure.

He felt his own gut clench nervously for Ralph as the boats began turning to come to the start, some five hundred yards upriver. They were small craft, easily pitched and rocked by the teasing of the lively Thames and getting them straight was no mean feat. It would be some time yet before they were off and

Edward allowed his eyes to wander. Where was Ginny?

Barely fifty yards away, Ginny was also scanning the crowds eagerly as they were jostled by the mass of happy race-goers.

'Looking for someone, Sis?' Mary teased at her side.

'No.'

A raised eyebrow was her sister's only reply. Ginny grinned at her sheepishly. Mary was looking lovely today. She had a new gown trimmed with pretty lace and a very becoming bonnet to protect her pale skin from the fierce sun on this first day of August. It wasn't just her outfit, though, Mary's eyes were shining and her skin glowed with health and happiness.

Every so often she would sneak glances across their smart little group and her lips would curve into a smile she was helpless to prevent, for, at their father's side, doing his best to be attentive but looking sick with nerves, was Nathan Johnson. He seemed very thin and angular next to bulky Josiah. He wasn't Ginny's idea of a man at all, but then no one for her could match up to Edward's quiet strength and easy assurance, but if Mary liked him then so much the better – as long as Josiah saw it that way.

'Enjoying yourself, Virginia?' her father boomed now. 'Come walk with me, girl, and give your old man an arm.'

He gestured ostentatiously to the opposite side from where Nathan was hovering. Not even daring to look at Mary, Ginny obediently moved to take her father's arm.

'Lovely day,' she managed.

'Isn't it!'

Josiah strode forward as if the crowds would part for him which, on the whole, they did. Ginny shot an apologetic smile at a young family that had been forced to scuttle aside but got little more than a grimace in return. She knew how their party must look in their smart clothes with their faces half hidden behind broad-banded bonnets, as if they were too good to be seen by all.

She had noticed Charlotte looking enviously at the local children running around, legs and heads joyously bare to the sunshine whilst she was hampered by her long skirts and her fancy parasol and she knew how her sister felt. She wouldn't change her family for the world and she loved them dearly but it seemed to her more and more recently that there was a price to pay for wealth. She was hugely grateful for the comfort of her life but the constraints of the nonsensical decorum that went with it could be too much to bear, especially when they kept her from the man she loved.

Just then, as if she had conjured him up with her thoughts, her eyes caught a wonderfully familiar fair head just a few yards away.

'Edward,' she breathed.

'Sorry, my dear?'

'Oh nothing Father. I was just, er, wondering how the rowers must feel right now. They must be very nervous.'

'Nervous?' Josiah considered, his florid head tipped on one side. 'I suppose they must.' He laughed and patted Ginny's hand. 'How tender of you to think of it, my dear!'

He glanced at Nathan, nodding pointedly as if a concern for watermen was some sort of wifely attribute. Ginny looked away, hiding her distaste. Her father had recovered fast from his sickness and was eating them out of house and home to 'catch up' on the meals he'd missed. Ginny had rather hoped this incident would frighten him into taking better care of himself, but Josiah seemed to have already forgotten he'd ever been ill. He lived life with a bullish optimism and relentless self-regard and, as he shouldered his way to the water's edge, ploughing unknowingly towards the Allerdice family group, Ginny felt suddenly ashamed.

'I think there might be a good space just down here,' she said, seeking to divert him but Josiah didn't even hear her.

''Scuse me,' he barked, nudging his stick against a young girl.

She swung round indignantly and glared up at him, her eyes fiery beneath tumbledown dark locks.

'I'm here,' she said.

'I beg your pardon?'

Josiah leaned forward, peering down at her as he might a curious insect that had just had the temerity to try and sting him. The girl shrunk back a little but stood her ground.

'I said I'm standing here if you don't mind, sir.'

'But I can't see the river properly.'

She frowned.

'Yes, you can. You can see over my head, but if you stand here I won't be able to see round you at all.'

Her eyes fixed pointedly on Josiah's bulging belly and Ginny felt, rather than saw her father's temper begin to boil.

'Mercy! Stand aside, dear.'

The girl's mother pulled her daughter towards her.

Mercy? Ginny knew that name. Her eyes, which she'd kept averted, crept upwards and there, just behind the feisty little girl, was Edward. Her face flushed and she tried to pour all her shame and apologies into her eyes but she was horribly aware that it wasn't going to be enough. What right did her father have to push a small girl out of the way?

'Father! Come away. They were here first.'

Josiah looked at Ginny then back to the Allerdices. He looked almost amused.

'So?' he said.

'So we have no right to take their place.'

'They're watermen, Virginia.'

Ginny's throat constricted with anger and mortification. From far away she felt Mary place a warning hand on her waist but she didn't care.

'They're people, Father, just like us.'

The Allerdices were all staring at her now, as if scarcely able to believe what they were hearing. Josiah was turning a livid shade of purple, the veins on his cheeks standing out like a map of his precious new world.

'Let's go somewhere else,' Ginny tried desperately.

'No, please. We can move.'

It was an older man who spoke now, with sun-dark skin and a rich head of salty grey hair. This must be Edward's father, Ginny thought, and beside him, still with her strong arms around her daughter, his mother. They looked open, friendly people although that was marred right now by the confrontation with her own family.

'Father, please. Look, the race is about to start.'

All around them people were straining forward and upriver the eight sturdy little sculls were in a tentative line, the rowers leaning forward, their oars dipped into the water ready for the off. Mercy pulled away from her mother and pressed herself to the low wall along the waterside.

'Our brother is racing,' she told Josiah over her shoulder. 'Look – there he is, right in the middle. Come on, Ralph!'

This last was yelled, her sharp little cockney voice carrying across the water. Josiah hesitated, but it was Nathan who calmly took his other arm and steered him past the Allerdices.

'Look sir, we can see very well from here and just in time – they're—'

His sentence was cut off by the sharp bang of the starter's pistol and the crowd went wild as the boats leapt forward. As people pressed against the wall, Ginny fell back behind her father and allowed herself to look for Edward. He was staring straight at her.

I'm so sorry, she mouthed, but he just smiled. Deep within the press of the crowd she felt him take her hand for a moment and when he withdrew it there was a tiny piece of paper nestling in her palm. Her fingers clenched over it as if it were gold dust and then she was swept past and all eyes were on the approaching rowers.

Nathan had managed to steer Josiah into a space on the bank and Mary had taken advantage of the crush to press in close to her beau. Josiah smiled down at her and made way for her at his side without so much as glancing round for his eldest daughter.

Ah well, Ginny thought, *at least if he's cross with me he might look more favourably at Mary marrying Nathan.*

Slowly, her heart in her throat, she unfolded Edward's note.

All Hallows, it said in his beautifully ill-formed hand. *Whenever you can make it after the race. I'll be waiting.*

Ginny read it swiftly then crushed it up and dropped it beneath the feet of the spectators where it would never be found. She glanced behind her to where the spire of the little local church poked jauntily up over the roofs of the squat riverside buildings and felt her heart start to beat with new strength. Soon she would see him alone. Soon she would be able to apologize properly. For now, though, the race was on and it seemed that Edward's brother was in the lead.

Chapter Fifteen

'Go on, Ralph!'

Edward felt his sides might burst with nerves and excitement as the boats drew level with the Allerdices' hard-won position on the bank. Ralph was in the lead by about a boat length but there was another lad hot on his tail and a third clearly not yet ready to give up the fight. They were at the halfway point and Edward could see the concentration on his younger brother's face as his strong young arms worked the oars with a fluid strength.

'He's holding them off,' he gasped to Nicholas. 'I'm sure he is.'

His mother's hands were clenched at her side. She was breathing fast and her eyes were shining with pride.

'He's doing so well. Go on, Ralph!'

All decorum – such as it ever was in their family – was forgotten now as with one voice they cheered their man on. And, as if he'd heard, Ralph seemed to respond with a renewed push. He was a length and half up now and didn't look in the mood to let anyone past.

'I'm going to follow,' Edward gasped. 'Come on, Nick.'

His little brother nodded and they detached themselves from the family to race along behind the crowds, straining to keep tabs on the boats as they ran. They weren't the only ones. It was a tangled and obstacle-strewn course but Edward didn't care. Somewhere behind him he could hear Lucy calling. 'Wait for me,' but right now he wouldn't wait for anyone, not even Ginny.

He felt a brief thrill of hope that he might see her later. She would be there if she could, he knew. She'd looked so beautiful all flustered over her father's blustering rudeness. Edward's chest tightened at the thought of the formidable man he was somehow daring to dream of as a potential father-in-law, but he pushed it aside. It was Ginny he wanted to marry not her family and, besides, now was not the time to concern himself with that.

'Go on, Ralph! Push! You're nearly there.'

Edward could see the finish line and hoped his brother knew how close he was. Ralph was still in the lead but the lad in second was pushing hard and Ralph's early effort was starting to tell. His head had dropped a little and he was clearly tired.

'Now, Ralph!' Edward all but screamed. 'Go now, lad!'

And somehow Ralph did. His head went up and he threw his broadening back behind the oars for a huge final few strokes. He went over the line just half a length up on his nearest rival, but it was enough.

'He won!' Edward punched the air and turned to lift a panting Nicholas up high to see. 'He won, Nick. Ralph won.'

All around them people, even those who didn't know him, were clapping him on the back.

'He's my brother,' he heard himself saying, stupidly proud. 'He's my little brother and he won the Doggett!'

'And we'll never hear the end of it,' Nicholas groaned, though happily.

Edward wasn't so sure. Ralph had been a changed man in these last couple of weeks and he was hoping this win would help him mature further, not turn him back into the cocky whippersnapper he'd been before.

'We have to see him,' he said. 'Come on.'

Together he and Nicholas snaked their way through the crowd towards the finish line where the racers were rowing slowly in to the rough landing stages. Edward scrambled down to the bank and virtually lifted his brother straight out of his craft.

'You did it, Ralph! You did it.'

'I did,' Ralph agreed but he looked more bemused than triumphant and his legs were shaking. 'Do you think I'd have beaten Gus?' he asked, his voice low.

'I'm sure of it. And he'd have been the first to congratulate you, all right?'

'All right, Brother.'

'Good. Now enjoy yourself. You deserve it.'

Others were descending on the winner now and Edward was happy to stand back and see him accept the congratulations of his friends and fellow racers.

'Gosh, Edward, you do run fast! I'm quite out of breath.'

Edward turned to find Lucy back at his side. He swallowed. He'd had a lucky escape the other night thanks to poor Sophie and her false alarm, but that was over and in the party that was bound to ensue this evening, Lucy was going to be harder than ever to avoid.

He felt a shiver at the thought of having to disappoint both her and his family. Was it worth it? And then he thought of Ginny waiting for him in All Hallows and knew that it was. He loved her in a way he could never love Lucy and surely that had to count for something? Best to speak to Lucy now, whilst they had a chance. Edward cleared his throat.

'Lucy, I—'

'Yes, Ned?'

She looked so hopeful. Edward sought for the right words but, before he could speak, Mercy bulleted into him.

'Where's Ralph, Ned? Have you found him? He did win, didn't he?'

'He did win,' Edward agreed, again relinquishing his 'chat' with Lucy with shameful ease. 'He's over there. In fact, look, they're getting ready to present the prize.'

Stephen and Eliza were here too now and the family were ushered forward as a space was cleared around a carefully erected platform. The mayor was taking the stage, his golden insignia glinting in the sunshine as he solemnly addressed the crowd about the glory of human endeavour.

'Human what?' Mercy demanded, tugging on Edward's sleeve.

'It means trying hard,' Edward told her.

'Well why didn't he just say that? They're all the same, these rich folks. Think they're so clever!'

Edward cringed but Ralph was being called to the stage now and all other concerns were banished from his mind as he watched his brother don the famous orange coat and have the winner's golden badge pinned to his lapel. He glanced at his father and Stephen nodded – he, like Ned, was thinking of the time not so many weeks ago that they'd walked out of the Waterman's Hall in disgrace with Ralph. How much he'd changed.

He was being ushered forward now to cries of 'Speech, speech!' Ralph put up a hand and the huge crowd fell silent.

'Thank you,' he said. 'I mean it. Thank you. Thank you to the organizers for providing this chance for the likes of us to be something a bit more than we might otherwise. And thanks to all of you for supporting us in it, especially for supporting me. I know there must be a few of you who think I'm not worth much. Maybe I wasn't – before – but I'm going to try to be now.'

He cleared his throat awkwardly and the crowd waited. Edward saw several of the elders exchanging impressed glances and felt even prouder of Ralph than before.

'I haven't much more to say,' Ralph went on, 'except another thank you to my wonderful family and to Perry's Sophie who persuaded me to go ahead and race. I want to dedicate this prize to Gus Richardson and his father. I wish they were here now and hope very much that they are looking down on us from Heaven. Thank you.'

And with that, Ralph turned and departed the stage as quickly as he'd taken it. Applause rang out around the waterside as Eliza and Stephen claimed him.

'He did well,' said Sophie at Edward's side.

Edward smiled at her.

'He did. Very well – thanks to you.'

'Thanks to himself. He's a strong character that one. He'll make a good man.'

Edward put an arm around her shoulders and gave them a squeeze.

'You bearing up, Soph?'

'I am, Ned, though I want it to come now really, whether Perry's back or not. If I can't hold him in my arms I want to hold his child.'

'You will,' he assured her. 'You soon will.'

She nodded sadly, then shook herself.

'Guess you'll be celebrating, hey? The Anchor?'

Edward shivered, remembering the horrors of the last time he'd been there and Perry had been snatched away by the impress.

'Not The Anchor. The King George perhaps. Father, the King George?'

Stephen waved acknowledgement over the crowd which was starting to move away now the race was over. Edward felt himself being tugged back and didn't resist. A man could get lost in this crowd for a little while, if he so chose. . . . Pausing only to make sure Sophie had someone to care for her, he ducked away and turned up a side alley, heading for the church of All Hallows.

'You came!'

'Of course. I said I wanted to give thanks for Father's recovery.'

Ginny rushed forward and let herself be drawn into a quiet corner behind the font. It was deserted inside the church with everyone else more intent on merry-making than prayers, but neither of them was prepared to take any more risk than they already had.

'I'm so sorry about my father,' she said, pressing herself against Edward. 'I was so ashamed.'

'He wasn't doing anything unusual. We're used to, um, men like him, wanting, well, precedence.'

Ginny laughed bitterly.

'Even you can't find a nice way of putting it. Rich folks throwing their weight around you mean. I'd never noticed it before and I don't like it. I won't be like that, not ever.'

'I know you won't, my love. It doesn't matter.'

'But it does, Ned. Your family will never approve of mine.'

He felt a surge of love for her. Unlike her father, Ginny took nothing for granted.

'They'll approve of *you*,' he said. 'Now hush a minute.'

'Why?' she asked, cheekily. 'Do you wish to pray?'

'I do,' he agreed, then pulled her against him, crushing his lips to hers. 'I pray,' he whispered onto her lips between kisses, 'for the rest of the world to see how perfect we are together. . . . I pray for you to love me forever . . . and I pray for the miracle of your father's consent to make you my . . . wife.'

Ginny felt she could stay here forever. Perhaps she could? Claim sanctuary in God's house as outlaws had once done, and refuse to come out until the priest had wed them. She put the idea to Edward.

'Tempting,' he agreed, clutching her even closer. 'Now that Ralph is reformed, the family needs a new troublemaker.'

He laughed and leaned forward to kiss her again but the reference to his brother had jolted her back to reality and she pulled away slightly.

'I'm sorry. I'm being selfish. You have to go and celebrate your brother's victory.'

'My brother will be quite happy. You needn't worry about him.'

'But your family will miss you.'

'Soon. Not yet. Don't go, Ginny.'

'I must. Martha and Charlotte are waiting outside for me and we have guests for dinner.'

'Not—'

'Nathan, yes.'

'He'll ask for your hand.'

She shook her head and dared to run her fingers up through Ned's hair.

'He won't. He's been making doe-eyes at Mary all day. He'll ask for her, I'm sure of it. Whether Father will say yes or not remains to be seen but he's already cross with me, so he might.'

'For standing up for our Mercy?'

She smiled at the possessive.

'For that, yes, but I'm still glad I did and will do so again.'

'For the rest of your life, Ginny?'

'If I have to. I love you, Ned, and I want to tell everyone.'

'I know,' he agreed. 'I know, Ginny. Things are getting awkward for me too.'

'They are?'

'There's a girl, my sister's friend. I think she's expecting, well . . .'

'No!' Ginny felt an ice-cold blade of purest jealousy, cut through her. 'What's her name? Have you known her long? Is she pretty?'

Edward looked down at her and smiled a slow, tantalizing smile that caught her breath.

'Her name is Lucy. I've known her since her birth and she's very pretty.' Ginny gasped, but he smothered it with his lips. 'But I feel nothing when I'm with her because I'm thinking of a woman one hundred times as beautiful, one hundred times as fiery, and one thousand times more important to me.'

'You are?'

'I am. My mother . . .'

'Edward!'

Ginny smacked at his chest but she was laughing now, the tension gone. Oh but this man was good for her! Nathan would never dare tease so. Above them the bells rang out suddenly, cutting through their merriment. Ginny glanced upwards fearfully.

'I have to go.'

'Me, too.'

'When will I see you again?'

'I'll call at the house. I said I would – about the insurance.'

'Yes. Oh yes, do. Soon.'

'I swear it. We'll work out a way of telling them, Ginny, I promise, just not yet. Let's bide our time, my love. We'll have the rest of our lives to walk together if we tread carefully now.'

She nodded, kissed him one last time and watched as he moved down the aisle towards the door. As it opened a shaft of golden light fell across him for a second and then he was gone. Ginny sighed and sank onto a nearby pew. In a few moments she would recover her public mask of 'dutiful daughter' and return home but she wanted just a little more time to savour the glory of the feeling between her and Edward. She closed her eyes.

'I saw you.'

'Charlotte!'

Ginny's eyes flew open again and she stared in horror at her little sister.

'I saw you with that fireman. That's who it was, isn't it? You were kissing him.'

'Where were you? How did you get in?'

'I was behind the font. Martha let me in to pray for Papa just like you, but you were too busy kissing to notice and I came through the door like any self-respecting church goer. You were just too busy kissing to notice. *Ooh Edward! I love you, Edward!*'

Charlotte rolled her eyes and clasped her hands to her heart in a melodramatic way. Ginny's blood started to boil but she forced herself to stay calm.

'You won't tell anyone, will you, Charlie?'

'Why not? Why shouldn't I, Ginny?'

'We haven't spoken to Father yet.'

'I bet you haven't. You can't mean to marry him, Gin? He's . . . he's poor.'

That did it. Ginny leapt to her feet, eyes blazing.

'He is not poor. He works very hard, harder than you or I ever will. He's solid and charming and intelligent and, and . . .'

'Poor,' Charlotte said, unperturbed by her sister's outburst. 'Father will never hear of it.'

'Father needn't know – yet.'

'Really? Is he a good kisser, Gin? Is it like in the fairy tales?'

'You've no right to . . .'

'Shall I ask Mother what she thinks, perhaps?'

'No!' Ginny took a deep breath. 'What do you want, Charlotte?'

The little girl considered.

'No bed til nine o'clock, sweetmeats every day and—.'

'And?'

'And three stories every night.'

'Not at nine o'clock.'

'Fine, then I shall have to tell my own. I tell good stories, you know, Gin. Did you hear the one about the rich man's daughter who—'

'All right, all right, but you had better keep quiet, Charlie, or I swear I'll . . .'

'You're in God's house,' her little sister reminded her impudently.

Ginny gritted her teeth.

'You're right and it's time we left. Come on, home with you and keep your mouth shut.'

'Of course,' Charlotte agreed, all sweetness now. 'Why wouldn't I? And you're right, Sis, we had better hurry up. Nathan Johnson will be waiting for you after all.'

Ginny cast a glance to the altar, praying for fortitude, then hurried to the door, dragging her impossible younger sister with her.

*

Outside the church, however, Edward had also suffered an ambush and not one that would be appeased with treats and stories.

'How dare you, Ned!'

He'd barely closed the door behind him before she'd stormed at him, hands on hips and eyes blazing with fury.

'Molly!'

'Who is she?'

'Who?'

'The girl. Who slid in after you. The fancy one with the maid waiting on her.' She gestured to the servant sitting on the step. Edward pulled her aside.

'You were spying on me?'

'No! At least, that wasn't my intention. I saw you slipping away and thought I'd take the chance to have a sisterly chat.'

'What about?'

'What about?' Molly spat. 'What do you think about? About Lucy, of course. My best friend, the girl you've been stringing along all these weeks.'

'I have not, Molly. I never said anything to her. I never made any promises or even gave her any indication that I liked her. It's all been you and Mother plotting between you – and well you know it.'

Molly paused but only for a moment.

'That's nonsense, Ned. You said you were ready to think about taking a wife and you've been looking all soppy and distracted recently, so I assumed you were, well, in love.'

'And I am.'

Edward sucked in his breath as the words leapt out. He'd said it. He'd admitted it and terrifying as that may be, it felt wonderful too.

'With . . .'

Molly waved a disparaging arm back towards the church door and, glancing over, Edward realized how soon Ginny might emerge. Taking his sister's arm, he hurried her quickly up the street. She protested furiously, trying to pull away but he wouldn't let her go until they were back on the riverside. The crowds were thinning now but there were still enough people about to stop Molly making too much of a scene – or, at least, so he hoped.

'Who is she?' Molly hissed.

'I'm not telling you.'

'Then I shall ask Father, shall I?'

'No!'

'She's rich though, isn't she? I saw her dress. I bet that cost as much as all mine, Mother's and Mercy's clothes for a whole year.'

'That's not her fault.'

'Ooh! You do like her, don't you?'

'Yes, I do. What's so bad about that?'

'You don't know?'

Edward hung his head. Of course he knew. It kept him awake late into the night and haunted his mind all the long working day.

'I'm not good enough for her.'

Molly softened.

'It's not that, Ned. You're wonderful, really, but this can't be. You're too different. Our families are too different. It would never work.'

'Why not? We're all people, aren't we? We all feel the same.'

'Not in our beds we don't – when we're on horsehair and they're on feathers. Not in our bellies – when we're scraping around the last of the turnip stew and she's picking at pheasant and glasshouse strawberries. This is madness, Ned, and you're going to break poor Lucy's heart with it, not to mention Mother's.'

The moment of softness had gone and Molly's anger was returning.

'Molly, please. Listen . . .'

But his sister spun away, nimbly evading his outstretched arm.

'I won't listen, Ned. You're betraying us all with this. I bet her father could make no end of trouble for the family if he finds out.'

'So don't tell.'

'What, and let you carry on? No, Ned, that's not fair. This is as dangerous to us all as that stunt Ralph pulled when racing Gus, and look where that ended up. I have to tell Father, and maybe he'll help you see sense.'

And with that, she picked up her skirts, dodged a group of carousing young men, and dashed off towards The King George leaving Edward lost and alone. The day had started so well but victory for the Allerdices was about to be turned to dust and ashes and all because of him.

'Oh, Ginny,' he muttered, casting his eyes across to the richer side of the water where for a few blissful weeks he'd dared to wander in his dreams. 'Whatever I just said, I think this might be goodbye, my love.'

Then he shoved his hands into his pockets, hunched his head down between his shoulders and went to face the music.

Chapter Sixteen

The King George public house was bursting with life as Edward approached. Racegoers were spilling onto the sunlit street enjoying a rare afternoon's leisure on one of the hottest days of the year. Girls stood giggling in groups as lads dared each other to approach. One was drawing himself a small crowd of admirers by juggling apples and another was enthralling with magic tricks.

Small children threaded their way through the forest of legs and the older generation looked on from chairs dragged out of the public house. Everyone looked happy. Voices shimmering with laughter rose on the warm air and the three rowers present were already reeling with the drinks that had been bought for them.

Edward edged forward nervously looking for his family. Had Molly got here ahead of him? Had she told them all about Ginny? Surely she wouldn't ruin their afternoon that way?

It'll be you that's done the ruining, he told himself sternly.

He couldn't blame his sister. She was only trying to act for the best but she didn't know what Ginny was like and she didn't understand how he felt about her. Perhaps if he could find her before she got to their parents he could have another go at explaining, but where were they all?

'You won't find your hero of a brother here,' someone said at his side.

Edward turned to see Sophie looking up at him, her face pink from the heat.

'Where is he?'

'Ceremonial dinner. He wanted to take you along but no one could find you, so your father went. Very proud he was.' She paused for a moment before adding softly: 'Where were you, Ned?'

Edward blushed.

'I got, er, pushed out by the crowd. Lost sight of you all.'

Sophie looked pointedly at his strong frame and broad shoulders.

'Pushed out, Ned?'

'All right, I escaped for a bit. Is it a crime?'

'I don't know. Depends where you escaped to.'

'Have you been talking to Molly?'

Edward glanced round anxiously for his sister and caught sight of her just down the street. She was talking away to someone: Lucy. Sophie followed his gaze and frowned.

'What's going on, Ned? Are you in trouble?'

'Probably,' he agreed gloomily.

He looked down at Sophie. She had a hand clutched to her bursting belly and looked hot and tired.

'Shall I take you home?' he suggested.

'Am I being too nosy?'

'No! You just look worn out. I promised Perry I'd take care of you and after the other night . . .'

She sighed.

'You're right, I know, and I do feel a bit uncomfortable but I'd like to see Ralph before I retire to my bed like the matron I seem to have become. You're avoiding my question, Edward.'

He grimaced.

'I know. I'm sorry. It's just, well, Mother and Mol expect me to marry Lucy and I think they've got Lucy expecting it too.' Sophie nodded. 'But I don't love her, Soph, not like Perry loves you. Not like—'

He caught himself before he went any further. This was dangerous talk.

'I'll walk you back,' he offered again, but at that moment a whirlwind in a pretty cotton frock whipped between them.

'Don't bother,' said an icy Lucy. 'I'll be happy to take Sophie home. I don't feel like a party anyway.'

Taking Sophie's arm, she fixed Edward with a piercing look full of disgust and scarcely hidden distress, then whirled away again, taking Sophie with her. The older girl glanced apologetically over her shoulder and then they were gone.

'Pleased with yourself, are you?' Edward snapped at Molly who'd come up beside him.

'Not at all, but someone had to break it to her and you were clearly too timid.'

'Not timid, Mol, just . . . considerate.'

'Ha! Good job for you Father isn't here.'

'Will you talk to him when he comes?'

'I might. You'll have to see how I feel.'

Edward shuddered, but at that moment a shout went up and he turned to see his father and Ralph coming towards them, Ralph glowing in his new orange coat and both of them beaming fit to burst. Several lads dashed forward to scoop Ralph onto their shoulders and bear him into the pub as everyone cheered and clapped. Edward glanced at Molly, pleading with his eyes for her not to spoil this moment. She snorted.

'Don't think you're getting away with this for more than an

hour or two, Edward Allerdice,' she warned then stalked off.

Edward felt relief run through him, but sadness crept in on its tail. He and Molly had always been close, always understood each other. Now it seemed he'd lost that – and this was just the beginning.

Ginny might be betrothed to Nathan by now anyway, he reminded himself grimly. The only wise thing to do this evening was to try and appease his own family.

'Oh! I'm sorry, I . . .'

Ginny hesitated in the doorway of the drawing room for, standing by the mantelpiece, fidgeting at the lapel of his smartest jacket was Nathan Johnson.

'Is it just you?' she asked nervously, glancing round.

'Just me,' he confirmed, his voice squeaky as he bowed to her.

Ginny cast a look back at the door but it was closed. Now she understood why her mother had been so keen for her to come downstairs.

Eliza Marcombe had been up and looking more sprightly than Ginny had seen her in weeks when they returned from the race earlier. Maids had been summoned, dresses chosen and hair coiffed. Ginny had been bored stiff and glad to escape downstairs at last, but now she felt trapped. Where was Mary? Or even Charlotte. This was the perfect time for the child's meddlesome attention-seeking. She glanced at the door again but no sisters appeared; clearly her mother was keeping them at bay. Taking a deep breath she crossed the room.

'I hope you're hungry, Nathan,' she managed. 'It sounded as if cook were planning a feast tonight.'

'Not very,' he said honestly.

Ginny relaxed a little.

'You're nervous?' she suggested.

He nodded.

'Me too,' she confessed and drew a little closer.

Nathan flinched. Ginny saw his Adam's apple bobbing in his throat as it worked its way round the words that were clearly lodged in there. She felt a dangerous flash of amusement.

'You may . . .' he stuttered, 'be expecting me to, well, erm, speak.'

'Speak, Nathan? Yes. It's usual at dinner, I believe.'

'Speak to you I mean, directly.'

'As you're doing now?'

'No. Well, yes, but . . .'

He was turning puce. She decided to be a little kinder.

'I never expect anything, Nathan. Being in business has taught me that whatever may appear to be going on, there is often more beneath the surface than you can ever know about.'

'There is? I mean, there is. Yes.'

'So I never expect anything until the contract is signed.'

'Contract?'

'In business.'

'Oh. I see. Business. Yes. And at, er, at home?'

'Much the same I suppose.'

He nodded keenly, though his eyes were still clouded with confusion. Ginny thought longingly of Edward's keen wit; this was like tormenting a helpless kitten. She took a deep breath and decided to put Nathan out of his misery.

'I know you and Mary have been getting on well of late.'

'Getting on. . . ? Well? Yes, yes we have. Getting on very well.'

'I think you like her, Nathan.'

'I do.'

'And I think she likes you, too.'

'Does she? Really? Are you certain.'

'As certain as I can be.'

'So you wouldn't mind if I, I . . . asked for her hand.'

'I'd be delighted,' Ginny confirmed, smiling as Nathan stood straighter before her.

'I'd be honoured to call you a sister, Virginia.'

'Ginny, please, and thank you, Nathan. I'd like that too. The only thing is . . .'

'Your father.'

'Yes.'

'He's expecting me to ask for you.'

'I'm afraid he is, but . . .'

'And he's not a man used to being gain said.'

'No, but . . .'

'I confess I am a little afraid of him.'

'Aren't we all? But Nathan, you must be brave. If you ask for Mary instead I will support you. Really I will.'

'Really?' Nathan leapt forward and clasped her hand. 'Would you do that for us, Virg– Ginny?'

'I—'

But before Ginny could speak further the door flung open and Josiah strode in. He took one look at the pair at the mantelpiece, hands clasped, and roared with laughter.

'Steady, young things, steady! Time enough for all that, hey!'

He was hugely pleased with himself but Ginny's heart sank as, behind his bulky form, she saw big, blue eyes take in the sight in the drawing room. Quickly she snatched her hand from Nathan's and moved towards her sister, but Mary had gone.

Dinner was a restless, awkward affair. Cook had indeed surpassed herself and course followed course. Neither Ginny,

Nathan nor Mary had much appetite but Josiah made up for all of them and Eliza ate surprisingly well too.

'I shall be delighted when autumn is upon us,' she announced over the salmon. 'I find the heat terribly oppressive. September is such a lovely month. Perfect for social events, don't you think, Mr Johnson?'

Nathan's father had arrived and was sitting to Eliza's right, looking a little overwhelmed by all the attention he and his son were receiving.

'Lovely,' he managed. 'My wife and I, God rest her soul, were married in September.'

'Quite right!' Eliza applauded.

Nathan's father glanced uncertainly at his son.

'Did you have many bridesmaids?' Charlotte piped up across the table.

She'd been taking advantage of Mary's distraction to sneak sips of wine. Her colour was high and her eyes dangerously bright. Ginny glanced at the clock. Almost nine, thank heavens – she'd be grateful when she could get her littlest sister safely upstairs, though that still left her middle one to deal with.

She'd tried to seize a moment with Mary on the way into dinner to explain about her time with Nathan but Mary had clung obstinately to Eliza's arm and refused to even look her way. Her shoulders, as she sat picking at her fish now, were stiff and her eyes downcast. Ginny knew her poor sister was steeling herself to have Nathan taken away and could hardly bear it. She hoped it would all come good when Nathan actually spoke to their father, though she was by no means sure of the young man's courage. If his nerve failed him she could find herself with a fiancé who didn't want her and a sister who hated her.

I won't let that happen, she vowed. *Nathan will marry Mary if I have to do the proposal myself!* But her heart sank at the thought of it. When on earth would dinner be over?

'The new boat will be ready for viewing in the dockyard next week, Father,' she said, seeking safer conversational waters.

'Lovely. Can't wait to get back to work. You must be worn out, my dear.' Josiah turned to Nathan. 'Ginny has been a saint whilst I've been ill. Tending me at my bedside and keeping the business afloat to boot. Clever lass, aren't you?'

'Just doing my job, Father,' Ginny said quietly, as Mary choked back a sob.

'Mary?' Josiah boomed. 'Was it a bone? I specifically told cook to make sure there were no bones. They're—'

'It wasn't a bone, Father.'

'Oh. Well, good. Stop spluttering then, girl, and finish up. Venison next, I believe.'

Ginny groaned and looked to the ceiling for strength.

'When I get married—' Charlotte started and something in Ginny snapped.

She leapt to her feet.

'You won't be fit to marry anyone unless you get your beauty sleep, young lady. I think it's bedtime for you.'

Charlotte looked like she might protest but Eliza provided some welcome support.

'Quite right, Ginny. I'll call the maid.'

She reached for her little bell but Charlotte was up now.

'I want Ginny to take me.'

'Virginia is eating, Charlotte,' Josiah said sternly.

'No, she isn't. She's barely touched her fish. There are poor people over the river who would kill for a piece of fish like that.'

'Charlotte! What is this nonsense?' Eliza demanded.

'Like that girl Daddy poked with his stick this morning. What

166

was her name? Mercy. She looked like she'd love a nice bit of salmon.'

Ginny pushed her chair out and shot to her sister's side. Charlotte was dangerous like this.

'I'll take her up,' she said quickly. 'She's had a very exciting day.'

'I'm not the only one,' the ten-year old said, but Ginny was propelling her from the room.

'I'll just settle her down with a quick story. Do, please, continue without me.'

Josiah looked torn between losing his prize daughter and fighting with his rebellious one. In the end he decided Charlotte was in danger of disrupting the happy family picture he was so enjoying putting across to the Johnsons.

'Quite right, my dear,' he said decisively. 'So good with children, my Ginny. Very maternal you know, Nathan.'

Blocking her ears to the rest, Ginny fled, dragging a protesting Charlotte with her.

Chapter Seventeen

'You asleep?'

'No. You?'

'Obviously not, stupid.'

Edward peered through the gloom to where Ralph was sitting up in the bed he shared with Nicholas. Their younger brother was flat out and snoring gently.

'You've had an exciting day,' Edward said.

'I suppose so. Plus, this lump of a lad is getting bigger all the time. When are you going to move out, Ned?'

'Don't you start!'

'Sorry. Feeling touchy, Brother? Lucy turn you down, did she?'

'No!'

'Then, what?'

Ralph's voice had softened and Edward felt something alarmingly like tears prickle in his eyes in response. He fought to stop them falling. Wasn't loving someone meant to make more of a man of you, not less? Perry had seemed instantly older and wiser the day he stepped out of the church door with Sophie on his arm, so what was going wrong with him? No church door perhaps?

'It's complicated,' he muttered.

'Try me. I can keep a secret you know. I've changed.'

'I know, Ralph. I know you have but this . . .'

How could he explain that this one was too much of a secret. Look what it had done to Molly already! She hadn't told Stephen tonight, but she'd only held off so as not to spoil what had been, for everyone else at least, a lovely night. Tomorrow would be different and Edward didn't want to have to face it. He dreaded disappointing his father, but he didn't want to let go of Ginny – not that she was his to let go of. Even now she might be at Nathan's side drinking whatever rich folks drank when they wanted to celebrate. Someone had been telling him the other day about some French wine with bubbles in. It cost more per bottle than their monthly rent.

Edward groaned and looked across at Ralph. It wasn't fair that he still had to share with Nick. He was a man now – and a man with honoured civic duties at that – he shouldn't be stuck in a nursery bed. It was time for Edward to move out one way or another. Perhaps he was the one who should be thinking about joining the navy.

'You all right, Ned?'

'Just wondering how Perry's doing. Where he is, you know, what he's seeing. D'you think it's good?'

'I think it's dangerous.'

'No more so than fighting fires.'

'But at least then you're at home.'

'Hmph,' Edward grunted. 'I might not be wanted much longer.'

'But—'

'Someone needs my bed,' he said pointedly.

'Fine, fine. If you want to be grumpy, you go ahead. I'm going to sleep.'

Ralph flung himself back down. The bed creaked in protest

and Edward smiled despite himself.

'I was proud of you today, you know,' he said.

'Yes, yes – start pandering up to me now,' Ralph snorted, but his voice was kind. 'Go to sleep, Ned. It'll all look better in the morning.'

Edward buried his head in the rough pillow and wished that could be true, but he felt sure that tomorrow was only going to look worse.

'You want to marry *who*?!'

Ginny, Mary and Eliza, sitting primly in the drawing room, coffee going cold at their sides, heard every word of Josiah's astonished outburst in the dining room next door. Mary looked at Ginny for the first time that evening and Ginny saw a fragment of hope steal into her eyes. It sounded as if Nathan had found some courage – but now what?

'Girls? What's going on?' Eliza demanded, but they were too busy straining to hear the men's talk to answer.

Tutting, their mother rose and shamelessly opened the door. Nathan's answer was much quieter and escaped even their keen listening, but there was no mistaking Josiah.

'But I had you down for Virginia. She's the eldest, you know. Brightest too.'

Ginny cringed but Mary didn't seem to even notice.

'Well, yes, Mary is a very gifted pianist,' Josiah conceded through the wall. 'Pretty too, yes. Yes, of course she is. Takes after her mother you know – she was a peach of a girl when I took her to the altar.'

Eliza simpered in the doorway but the present was far too captivating to dwell for more than a second in the past, however golden. Josiah's next words rang out even louder:

'You do?'

All three women exchanged glances.

'He does what?' Mary whispered.

'Love you, I expect,' Ginny told her, longing to laugh.

Her father didn't sound angry, not really, just confused. She crossed the fingers of one hand and with the other, reached out and took Mary's.

'But earlier . . .' Mary whispered.

'Earlier, you silly thing, I was telling Nathan I'd support him all the way in asking for your hand.'

'You were? Oh, Ginny, I'm sorry. I—'

'Ssh. Father's speaking again.'

Mary bit her lip and strained forward, her fingers gripping tight to Ginny's.

'Well it's all a bit of a surprise,' Josiah was saying. 'You young people, hey! Full of your own ideas.' They could hear him blustering as he processed the information. 'But won't Virginia be terribly disappointed?'

There was a pause.

'Did she indeed? She's getting too independent for her own good, that one. Maybe you made a wise choice, young man. Mary's a very biddable girl. Caring too and with a lovely eye for a soft furnishing so her mother says. Yes, you'll probably have less trouble with that one.'

Mary glanced at Ginny, concern in her eyes, but Ginny was trying hard not to laugh.

'In fact,' Josiah's voice went on, growing in confidence with every second, 'I think Mary would be much better suited to you all round, so if you have no objection . . . No? Good, good.'

Hope lit in Mary's eyes as her bluff father skilfully turned the whole plan into his own, inspired idea. She leapt to her feet as her mother gently closed the door.

'Sit down, girl, sit down. Look modest!' Eliza commanded but Mary was past modesty now.

Her feet were twitching and her eyes sparkling as the men arrived. She flew to Nathan who was grinning from ear to ear as he dared to take her hand and Josiah announced their engagement to the room – and probably half the street too, Ginny thought ruefully.

Josiah glanced at Ginny, concern in his eyes and she knew she'd be cornered for a 'chat' later but for now she smiled and clapped and accepted a glass of the champagne Josiah ordered up from his cellar as if nothing was wrong at all. And, indeed, she had no desire to marry Nathan Johnson, though she couldn't help a niggling feeling that her own engagement, if it ever came, would not be embraced in this joyous way.

Mary's hidden romance was one thing, but if Josiah found out about Ginny's secret love she was more likely to end up where the sparkling wine had come from. Swallowing her drink with difficulty, she glanced nervously at the ceiling and prayed that Charlotte would stay asleep, preferably for about the next three months.

But no one was to sleep more than three hours that night. The Allerdices were the first to be woken, at just gone midnight, by a hammering on their door. Edward, still restless, was first to get there and found Lucy outside. He blinked in astonishment, then his brain caught up.

'Sophie?'

Lucy nodded, her eyes averted from Edward's but this was no time for petty differences.

'I'll get dressed.'

'Be quick, Ned. She's really struggling this time.'

'Is Midwife Jones there?'

'No! She's with Sarah Richardson from Church Street. Been at it for hours she has and she's weakening something dreadful. Midwife can't leave her for even a minute.'

'But Sophie . . .'

'I know!'

The rest of the family were appearing now. Ralph handed Edward his trousers, Maud filled their arms with towels and bowls and they went out of the door after Lucy.

'I'll be there in a minute,' Maud called.

'But, Mother . . .'

'But mother nothing. I've had five children, Ned, so I'll be more help than the rest of you put together.'

But she wasn't. Sophie was clawing at the walls of her little cottage as the pains tore at her and no one knew what to do. Edward and Ralph hovered awkwardly at the doorway, one eye on the road for the midwife, the other on the wild-eyed, wretched Sophie. Lucy was getting increasingly anxious, Molly was bewildered, and Maud, whose broad hips had given her little more than the usual trouble in birthing, was uncertain what to do with the tormented young mother.

'I'm being ripped apart,' Sophie wailed. 'Where's Midwife Jones? I need her. It's not right. It doesn't feel right. I want Perry!'

She collapsed, sobbing, her usual calm eaten up by the pain. Edward moved towards his best friend's poor wife, but Ralph got there first.

'I'm going to die, Ralph, aren't I?' she gasped, clutching at him. 'Perry will come back and I'll be dead.'

'Rubbish. That's rubbish, Sophie.' Ralph pressed his forehead to Sophie's. 'It's like I was in the race. This is the dark bit where you think you're going to fall apart, but you're not. I didn't and you won't. You know you won't. You're so strong, Sophie.'

Edward's heart wrenched at his brother's words but a long, tortured wail from Sophie cut through them. Edward's thoughts leapt to the one person he could think of who might know what to do.

'I know someone who could help,' he blurted out.

'You do?'

Molly looked up at him, yesterday's argument forgotten in the horror of the night.

'She's not a midwife but she knows medicine. I'll fetch her, shall I?'

Molly didn't even hesitate.

'Fetch her, Ned. And quickly.'

Chapter Eighteen

It wasn't easy getting Ginny's attention. Ned knew her room looked out onto the herb garden at the back. He let himself in the side gate he'd first walked through just a few long weeks ago and eyed the windows. She'd given the impression she was up on the first floor which gave him a choice of two windows. There was no time to hesitate. Taking a deep breath, he picked one, found a small stone and threw it. It clattered gently against the glass but nothing happened. He found another and threw it again, his legs poised to run if the dreaded head of Josiah Marcombe should appear.

A light flickered. Another stone and the curtain drew back a little. It was a brightly moonlit night and Edward dared himself to stand on the open path so that Ginny, if it was Ginny, could see him. The window flew up and he braced himself but there she was – her dear face haloed with loose, tumbledown hair that almost took his breath away.

'Ned? Are you all right?'

Her voice was little more than a whisper but it carried on the still summer air.

'I'm fine, but my friend – Sophie – she's in trouble, Ginny.'

'The babe?'

He nodded.

'Is there no midwife?'

'Busy.'

He saw her consider but only for the tiniest moment before she whispered, 'Wait there', and withdrew.

Minutes later, he heard the latch rise on the little herb room door and she appeared, her dress askew and her hair hastily caught up beneath a little cap. She was clutching a basket full of bottles and pots as she stepped out.

'Show me the way.'

Edward felt afraid suddenly. What had he done? He was endangering her. It was reckless of him, cruel even, and certainly ungentlemanly. What must she think?

'Are you certain? I shouldn't have—'

'Show me the way, Edward.'

So he did. Together they threaded through the deserted streets, their feet falling in time, both quietly aware of the other's proximity. They crossed the bridge, their figures casting brief, flickering shadows on the swirling silver water far below before they reached the other side and plunged into the maze of narrower streets. Edward's feet picked up pace as they got closer to Sophie's house, his heart beating faster too as he prayed they were in time.

Ginny's breathing quickened a little, but she did not object and she was still able to step calmly into the house when they finally arrived. Sizing up the situation in an instant, she stepped forward and took Sophie's arm.

'I'm Virginia,' she said, 'and I'm here to help you.'

'Help me die in peace?'

'No, I'm going to help you deliver this baby and live to nurse it until it totters away to play. My mother nearly died birthing my little sister, but I wouldn't let her and I won't let you either.'

'But I can't do it,' Sophie told her, looking into her eyes.

Ginny looked straight back, as if they were the only two people in the world.

'You can and you will. What we need first is some space. You walk around all you like. Would you mind stepping back a bit?'

She turned for the first time to the other women who obediently moved to the edges of the room, grateful for Ginny's apparent authority. Edward watched in pride and hope, his heart in his mouth. Ginny looked at Molly.

'Would you mind fetching a cup? I have a draught that should ease the pain.'

Molly nodded and ran.

'And a shawl or something? Sophie's cold.'

Indeed, she was shivering despite the warmth of the night. Lucy ran to fetch one.

'And a warm, damp cloth? Please?'

Now Maud was gone, grateful to be of use. Ginny turned to Edward and Ralph.

'You two – out! This baby doesn't need men about the place.'

Ralph's eyes widened. He followed Edward into the street without comment, but once outside he turned to him.

'I can see why you can't sleep, Brother.'

Edward grinned ruefully.

'None of us is sleeping tonight.'

Together they looked at the window where they could still hear Sophie labouring, then turned together to pace the street before the little house in tense silence.

'It's breech,' Ginny gasped, what felt like an eternity later. 'That's why it hurts so much, Sophie. Your baby is the wrong way round.'

'What?'

'It's all right. It'll be all right. It's coming. It won't hurt for longer, I promise. Just a few more pushes.'

Ginny tried to keep her voice calm, remembering all that the old herb lady who'd nursed her mother had taught her. They'd often sat long into the night discussing different medicinal matters and the problems of birthing had been one of the old lady's favourite subjects.

'We're just not designed right,' she'd say, shaking her head. 'Too upright we are. Should be more like the animals – just popping them out without much more than an intake of breath.'

It used to make Ginny laugh but it was no laughing matter now. Sophie's life – Edward's friend's life – was in her hands and that of her babe too. If she did this wrong . . .

You can't do it wrong, she told herself sternly and crouched down, murmuring words of encouragement as another pain came.

'Push, Sophie. Now – but slowly!'

The girl was weak after a night of travail but she pushed all the same and suddenly the baby was coming, first one little leg free and then the next.

The cord, Ginny reminded herself, feeling for it. *We have to beware of the cord.* If it wrapped around the baby's neck every push would strangle it. Her fingers found it, still safely to one side and she closed her eyes and prayed for help from the Lord.

'It's coming. It's really coming, Sophie. One more push.'

Sophie let out a heartrending wail, but was silenced just a few seconds later by another smaller but altogether more insistent cry.

'My baby?' she gasped, not daring to believe it.

Ginny nodded, tears in her own eyes.

'It's a boy, Sophie. It's a beautiful baby boy and he looks very, very well.'

Carefully Ginny lifted the baby, shivering at the miracle of the new life in her hands, and placed it into Sophie's waiting arms. The baby kicked out, his little foot tangling in the cord that bound him to his tearful mother. Ginny blinked the emotion out of her own eyes – there was still work to be done to ensure Sophie came out of this night as healthy as her son. She struggled to remember what to do next and felt quite ridiculously grateful when the door opened and a large woman bustled in.

'Looks like my work is done here,' she commented with a smile.

'Not quite,' Ginny said, and rose shakily to let Midwife Jones take over.

She glanced around her and was horrified to see dawn creeping in through the window. She had been gone all night and already the maids might be rising at home.

'I must go,' she gasped.

Sophie held out a hand.

'Thank you. Thank you so much. I was so helpless.'

'You were not,' Ginny said hotly. 'You were brave and strong, unbelievably so. That must have been agony.'

Sophie just smiled.

'But it isn't any more,' she said. 'I'm so grateful. I hope I'll see you again to thank you properly.'

'I hope so too,' Ginny agreed in a half whisper and then she fled.

As she opened the door Ned and Ralph jumped forward.

'It's a boy,' Ginny told them. 'A perfect little boy.'

'And Sophie?'

'Is well, I think. I'm no expert.'

'You're wonderful,' Edward said, taking her hands as Ralph slipped inside. 'Really, I can't believe how—'

'Ned, I need to go.'

Ginny looked to the sky and he nodded agreement. As they were about to leave, however, Molly came running out.

'I want to thank you too, Virginia,' she said. 'Please? If you'll let me. I know who you are and I know what you are to Ned.' She glanced awkwardly at her brother but stood her ground, 'and I want to say that I was wrong to judge you just because of, well, your dress.'

'My dress?'

'I'm sorry. I wish you well. Both of you. You know, together . . .'

Molly had turned scarlet now. She darted forward and planted a quick kiss on Virginia's astonished cheek before ducking away as quickly as she'd come. Ginny's hand went to her face as she stared at Edward.

'My sister. She's a bit mad.'

'She's lovely.'

'She means well. Come. We'd better get you home.'

The streets were coming to life as Ginny and Edward walked back over the river together. They were scared now that there was no comforting blanket of night to hide their identities and were both breathing hard by the time they turned into Paradise Street.

'I'll be safe from here,' Ginny said. 'You'd better go.'

'You're sure?'

'Sure. I'll slip into bed and no one will be any the wiser.'

Edward took a step back. Ginny knew she had to go inside – every minute they lingered was dangerous – but she couldn't stop herself reaching towards Ned again. For one night she'd seen into his world and it hadn't put her off; rather it had fed her longing to know more about this man she couldn't stop herself loving.

'Thank you for fetching me,' she said softly.

'Thank you for coming. Oh Ginny, I didn't think I could love you more than I did, but I was wrong. I can't wait to see you again.'

'Or I you.'

The clatter of boots on back steps somewhere behind them, made them both jump.

'Go,' Edward urged, 'and stay safe, my love. I'll call very soon. We'll be together soon.'

'Soon,' she echoed wistfully and then she fled, his words tingling through her tired brain as she slipped down the passage at the side of the house and lifted the latch on the back door.

She stepped quietly inside, depositing her basket beneath the big table in the herb room before heading for the stairs. It was a good job Martha was such a lazy so-and-so. She'd be in her room before anyone even knew she'd gone. She grabbed the banister to keep her weight from creaking on the stairs and went upwards, but, as she reached the second landing, she froze in horror. Standing before her, hands on hips and fury in his eyes was her father.

'Where do you think you've been, young lady?' Josiah roared. 'And who the hell is this fireman Charlotte says you've eloped with?'

Chapter Nineteen

'I'm sorry, Ginny. I'm so, so sorry. I didn't mean to get you into trouble, really I didn't. I just heard you go out and I was so scared. I thought you'd gone. I thought you'd left us and, oh Ginny, I don't want you to leave us. You won't leave us, will you?'

'Hush now. Of course I won't.'

Ginny put her arms around her barely coherent little sister and rocked her soothingly. She couldn't blame Charlotte. It had been too much to expect a ten year old to keep Edward a secret. Instinctively she started singing a lullaby to get the little girl back to sleep. She felt Charlotte relax in her arms but her own mind was far from calm.

Ginny glanced fearfully at the door, worried that Josiah might storm in and start ranting at her again. For well over half an hour she'd had to stand in the stairwell listening to her father's furious diatribe about her impudence, her lack of consideration, and her defiance. She'd had to listen to him blame himself for giving her too much freedom, her mother for never being out of bed to teach her proper manners, then finally – and mainly – herself for being a 'wanton little hussy not deserving of the precious name of Marcombe'.

She hadn't dared defend herself, hadn't dared say anything to fuel the already out of control flames of her father's anger, so she'd just stood there with Charlotte clutching at her skirts, and Mary looking terrified at her left shoulder, and Martha snickering at the bottom of the stairs until he had finally run dry. He hadn't finished with her, though, she knew that: he was merely gathering energy for a further onslaught.

The door handle turned and Ginny cringed back. Charlotte, sensing her tension, awoke again instantly and whimpered, but it was not their father who stepped into their room but, to Ginny's surprise, their mother.

'Are you well, Virginia?' Ginny bit her lip, uncertain how to answer what might easily be a trick question. Eliza came closer. 'No, really, Ginny. Are you well? Has anything bad happened?'

She sat on the side of the bed. Charlotte quietened and Ginny shifted a little to see her mother properly. Eliza was pale and looked genuinely concerned.

'Nothing bad has happened, Mother, and I am quite well, thank you. I was just asked to attend a girl in labour, that's all.'

'In labour? You? But why?'

'The midwife couldn't be there and the poor girl was having terrible troubles.'

'As I did with this little one?'

She leaned over to pat Charlotte's leg.

'Similar, Mother. The baby was breach but he is safely born now.'

'And the mother?'

'The mother seemed good too. Happy. But I had to leave very soon after the birth. I wanted to get home without . . . without worrying any of you.'

'You didn't manage it.'

'No.'

The two women shared a glimmer of a smile and for the first

time in ages Ginny saw her mother as something more than just a patient. Eliza cleared her throat.

'Who called for you, my love?' Ginny didn't answer. 'Was it this fireman Charlotte saw you with?'

'Perhaps. I—'

'Who is he, Ginny? Who is this man you care so much for?'

Ginny longed to confide in her mother but she didn't dare to speak Edward's name. It would go back to her father and then he would be in trouble and she didn't want that. She shook her head and Eliza sighed.

'Your father is very angry, Ginny, and rightly so. Anything could have happened to you. Ladies of your rank don't go rushing around the streets alone at night.'

'But I wasn't alone!'

'I see. So it *was* him, then? You're too trusting, Daughter. A man like that – he could be as much of a danger to you as anyone.'

'Edward would never harm me!'

It was out before she could snatch it back. Her mother just raised an immaculate eyebrow and for a moment Ginny thought she'd go running to Josiah but then Eliza surprised her by throwing her thin arms around her and squeezed her surprisingly hard.

'I've been in love, my dear, and so has your father. He won't stay angry for long. Not with you.'

Ginny's heart started to race. Was it going to be all right? Would her parents listen to her?

'And then what?' she dared to ask.

'And then he'll forgive you.'

'And I might be able to . . . to introduce Edward to him?'

Eliza pulled back.

'The fireman? Don't be silly, darling.'

'But then–'

'You'll have to forget him, Ginny, and you will. Soon it will be as if this unfortunate little incident had never even been. I'll help you find someone new to love, someone suitable.'

'Suitable?' Ginny yanked herself out of her mother's cloying grasp and leapt up. 'I don't want to love anyone else. I don't want to be suitable. I want to be me and I can best be me when I'm with him.'

Eliza looked shocked but rallied with the ease of the well-born society lady.

'I know it feels that way at the moment, darling, but–'

'No buts. I'll marry Edward or I'll marry nobody.'

Charlotte's eyes were wide at this drama in her very own room as Eliza stood, her shoulders tight and her lips pursed.

'I'm afraid that's not for you to say, Virginia my dear. You are a woman and as such you will do what you are told.'

'Why? Because that's all we're fit for? Really Mother, are you happy to take that? Are you happy to be second best, to prop up some man instead of being a person in your own right? Because I'm not. Father knew that and he supported me in it but now, when it counts, he's turned on me. I wasn't going to elope. I wasn't going to walk out on my own family – my own family whom I love dearly – but I might now, because clearly they don't love me.'

Eliza looked pointedly to the ceiling for patience.

'You're being melodramatic, darling. You're tired and over-wrought. It will look better in the morning, believe me.'

Ginny scowled. 'It is the morning, Mother, and it's never looked worse.'

Eliza tossed her head. 'Fine then, Virginia, be stubborn, but you are not leaving this house until you change your mind. Not in the day and most certainly not in the night.'

She swept out leaving Ginny quivering with rage and Charlotte in tears.

'You can't elope, Ginny,' she quavered. 'You said you wouldn't leave me.'

'And I won't,' Ginny agreed sadly, sitting back down on her sister's bed to draw her in for a cuddle, 'but I can't just let them have it their own way. They can't just brush this "unfortunate little incident" under the carpet as if it never happened. This is important to me.' She clasped her little sister's hands. 'You have to do something for me, Charlie.'

'Anything,' the little girl agreed valiantly, although she was struggling to stay awake now.

'You have to get a note to Edward. I'll tell you where to send the messenger. He has to know what's happened so he stays away. If he comes here again Father might kill him.'

'Kill him?'

Ginny took a careful breath.

'Not *kill* him. Of course not. Just, er, shout at him. A lot.'

'Like he did to you?'

'Like he did to me,' Ginny agreed heavily. 'Will you do it, Charlie?'

'"Course I will.'

And, as the girl slid into sleep at last, Ginny knew that this was the most co-operation she was going to get in her home for some time to come.

'Ned. You came!'

'Of course I did, Sophie. Here.'

Edward thrust the meadow flowers he was carrying at his

friend's wife but as she reached out a hand to take them, he was surprised to see that she was shaking.

'Sophie? What's is it?'

'Nothing. It's nothing. Just, you know – tiredness and that.'

'But you're trembling.'

'I know. I've been feeling strange all day. Scared almost, as if everything is going to go wrong somehow.'

Edward darted forward.

'But it isn't, Sophie. You're doing brilliantly and the little lad is, too – isn't he?'

Sophie looked down at the tiny baby clutched to her chest and managed a smile.

'He's wonderful,' she agreed, but even as she said it, tears were leaking from her eyes.

Edward patted her knee awkwardly and offered his handkerchief.

'I'm sorry,' she said. 'I'm being silly. Midwife Jones says everyone gets like this around this time. Girl's stuff, you know? Oh Lucy, thank you.'

Edward jumped back as Sophie's young helper came into the room with an earthenware vase.

'Good evening, Lucy,' he said politely, but got little more than a grunt in reply.

Lucy put the flowers roughly into the pot, placed them on the table and then turned to Sophie, pointedly ignoring Edward.

'Will you be all right if I nip out for a while?' she asked.

'I'll look after her,' Edward offered, but Lucy didn't even glance his way.

'That will be fine, Lucy,' Sophie said softly. 'Thank you.'

'Have a nice time,' Edward tried again, as Lucy went to the door but she just tossed her hair and was gone.

Edward hung his head.

'She's just making you suffer, Ned.' Sophie said with a glimmer of a smile at last. 'The amount of free mussels we've been getting, I'd say the fishmonger's boy is making sure our Luce doesn't feel too unloved. Now, come and sit down and say a proper hello to Percival junior. It's so good to see you.'

Edward nodded and pulled up a stool to look at the baby, now four days old and clearly thriving. Percy nestled in the crook of Sophie's arm, his eyes peacefully shut and little lips moving as if he were talking away to someone only he could see.

'He's lovely, Sophie.'

'Isn't he? I can't imagine what I ever did without him and I can't wait for his father to see him. He'll be so proud.'

'Have you written?'

'Of course. The very first morning. I sent it to the naval offices as usual, but I don't suppose Perry will get it for weeks.' Sophie's voice wobbled dangerously. 'I wish I knew where he was, Ned – and I wish it was here.'

'He'll be sorry to have missed all the drama, that's for sure.'

Edward attempted a grin, but it wasn't returned by his friend's wife and then, as a knock sounded at the door, she clutched at his arm.

'Who's that?'

'I'm not sure. I'll go, shall I?'

Sophie nodded but didn't let go of his arm and he had to prise her free to rise. He opened the door to see a young lad standing on the step proffering an envelope. He glanced back at her.

'It's just a letter, Soph.'

'A letter? Who from? What does it say?'

'Steady on, girl. I've no idea yet.'

'Is it black round the edges?'

'Black? No. Oh Sophie, no it isn't.' He reached out a hand to take it from the messenger. 'It looks rather smart actually. Oh and it's . . . it's for me!'

'Mr Edward Allerdice, sir?' the lad asked.

'That's right.'

'That's good then.'

He thrust the letter at Edward and, with a glimpse from left to right, was gone. Edward stared after him bemused but then his eye caught the handwriting on the rich cream envelope and his heart turned over.

'Ned? Who's it from, Ned?'

He swallowed.

'It's all right, Soph. It's for me.'

'You?'

'Strange, I know, but true.'

Already he was tuning out from his friend's little front room as he carefully broke the wax seal and revealed the precious words inside. He crossed to the window to catch the last of the day's light, noticing, as he did so, his brother's head passing outside. There was a knock on the door and Sophie jumped again, but Edward let Ralph in with barely a hello. He heard his brother cross to Sophie and murmur to the baby as he opened the letter but then it was as if Ginny's voice was in the room as he slowly read her words.

My dearest Edward,

I hope this reaches you safely and that Sophie and the babe are well. Please give them my best wishes. I wish that were the sole purpose of this note, but it is not, for I must warn you not to come near me. Not out of my own choice (given that, you would never leave my side) but for your safety, which is very dear to me.

My father discovered my absence last night and is in a mighty rage. I am confined to the house, not allowed out for work or for fresh air. I am even banned from my precious garden and have no idea how long his anger against me will last. I have not told him who you are and I beg you to stay away from the house for both our sakes. I do not give up hope for us, my love, but for now we must be apart.

Take care and pray for . . .

Here the beautiful handwriting faltered and smudged before concluding:

For a miracle. Yours for ever,

Virginia

Edward stared at the note in horror. He read it again and again, desperately hoping that it was his poor literacy making him misinterpret the words, but there was no denying them. It had happened. They had been discovered and they were in trouble – how could it ever have gone any other way?

He wasn't aware he was groaning until Ralph grasped his shoulders and shook him.

'Edward? What is it?'

Edward held out the note but Ralph shook his head – his reading was worse than Ned's.

'Is it Ginny?' Sophie asked gently.

Edward nodded and turned to them.

'Her father caught her creeping back in the other night. He's furious and she's confined to the house.'

'Oh no! Oh poor Ginny – and it's all my fault.'

'Nonsense, Sophie. It would have happened sooner or later and Ginny would never blame you. She even sends her best wishes.'

'And you, Edward? Do *you* blame me?'

Her eyes filled with tears again and he went to her side.

'No! Of course not, Sophie. This trouble is not of your making. It's ours – mine and Ginny's – and it seems it's about the only thing we might ever get to share.'

'Except love?'

Edward's face softened.

'Except love and better to have at least had a taste of that than not, hey?'

'I suppose so,' Sophie agreed softly, 'but for myself I'd prefer a feast.'

Edward smiled.

'And you will have one, I'm sure. Perry will be home soon. God knows, we all pray for that.'

Sophie shivered.

'Don't, Ned. Don't say that.'

'But—'

'I have a bad feeling. I've had it all day.'

'It's just girl's stuff, Sophie – remember? It'll pass.'

Sophie, however, rose, the baby clutched to her, and paced the tiny room. Edward and Ralph exchanged worried looks and Ginny faded a little from Edward's mind.

'Perhaps you should go to bed, Sophie? Get some sleep.'

She rounded on them.

'I can't sleep. I can't sleep without Perry here. I want him back. Ned. I want—'

But what Sophie wanted was cut short by a quick rap on the

door. Sophie stared at it, fixed to the spot. Ralph stared at Sophie and it was left for Edward to answer once more. He flung open the door, expecting a well-wisher, but knew the moment he saw the lad, satchel over his shoulder and fear in his eyes, that Sophie was right to be afraid. This was no girl's stuff. This was men's business and the rough little letter the lad was holding out as if it might bite him, had black all around the edge. His hand shaking, he took it and watched the messenger scamper away.

'No,' Sophie whispered, clutching at Ralph. 'Oh, please no.'

Hardly daring to breathe, Edward pulled the rough envelope apart. Sophie's own joyful note describing the arrival of baby Percival fell out and they all stared at it on the floor between them.

'Read it, Ned. You have to read it.'

Sophie was stroking her baby's head over and over, faster and faster, her eyes fixed on Edward and the dreaded letter. Edward did as she asked, his voice only halting a little on the hated words. The letter was short and stiff with formal regret. The clerk in the naval office had managed to add his sorrow at the timing of the news to the information that Perry's ship had been sunk in battle out at sea and the whole crew were presumed dead.

'No!'

Sophie's wail rent the air and her poor fatherless baby started awake and added his innocent cries to hers. Shoving his own now banal-seeming note from Ginny deep into his pocket, Edward rushed to join Ralph at her side as Sophie sank to the floor in despair.

Chapter Twenty

'Virginia?

Ginny looked up from the dressing table where she and Mary were poring over a list of wedding guests whilst Martha arranged Mary's hair. It was far from her own choice of activity but she was restless and in need of diversion after so much time cooped up at home so had turned her mind to arranging her sister's nuptials.

'Just completing Mary's guest list, Father. Very important to get it right, I think.'

'Yes. Absolutely. You look lovely, Mary.'

Mary beamed.

'Thank you, Father.'

They were due to dine with Nathan's parents and Mary was, indeed, glowing with the excitement of it all.

'We'll be ready to go out in an hour or so, my dear,' Joseph continued to her, avoiding Ginny's eye, 'but in the meantime, if you can spare her, I would like to ask Virginia a couple of things about the business.'

'The business?' Ginny questioned tightly, tipping her head on one side as if the business was an alien concept to her.

She was still worried about what Josiah might do, especially if he found out Edward's name and address, but a week of domestic activities had sharpened her temper.

'Please?'

A kick under the table from Mary forced Ginny to stand and follow her father into his study. He showed her in like a guest, closed the door more quietly than was his wont, and then shuffled awkwardly before her.

'A glass of wine, my dear?'

'No, thank you, Father. You wanted to talk about the business?'

'Yes. I hoped you might come back to Marcombe's tomorrow.'

'Is that allowed?' she asked frostily.

'Ginny, please – you cannot think that I could let behaviour like yours go unpunished, surely? If nothing else, I was worried about you. Charlotte was screeching like a banshee about some man carrying you off and you have to admit you were gone a long time.'

'On women's work, Father. Herbal work.'

He grunted.

'I know – your mother told me – but that's beside the point. Are you denying that there is a man? Are you telling me that you have not been courting someone from the other side of the river?'

Ginny took a deep breath. It was time to be honest, time to appeal to her father's sense of fairness.

'I have met someone, Father and, yes, he lives on the other side of the river, but so what? It's not so far away surely?'

'It's a million miles away. Might as well be the Indies. What does he do, this chap?'

'He's a fireman, you know that.'

'Yes. He came to the house apparently – in the drawing room with you all alone according to Martha. That's not right, Virginia, and you know it.'

'He was telling me about fire insurance. It's important you know. If a fire—'

'Virginia, really! If I want fire insurance I shall sort it out myself without your beau insinuating his way into my home, but this is beside the point. What's this man's real job when he's not playing at being a hero?'

Ginny gasped.

'He doesn't *play* at being a hero, Father. It's a dangerous profession and he's a brave man.'

'But not a rich one. What's his real job, girl?'

Ginny hung her head.

'He's a lighterman.'

'A lighterman? A lighterman – good God! Now I remember you nagging on about some lighterman before, but how on earth did you meet him?'

'I met him when you took me on board his boat with Nathan and his father. We got talking and, and . . . we've only met a couple of times, Father, and only ever in public.'

Ginny crossed her fingers desperately behind her back. It had been in public – the church, the woods, the streets – there just hadn't been anyone else around.

'So how on earth can you want to elope with him? Are you out of your mind?'

Ginny pulled herself up tall.

'I do not want to elope with him, Father. I want to marry him with your blessing.'

'My. . . ?'

'And I'm not out of my mind. I love him.'

'Love him?!'

Josiah was turning purple with rage and incomprehension.

'Yes, Father. Surely you know how that feels?'

It was Josiah's turn to pull himself up straight. He stepped closer to Ginny and peered down at her, so close that she could see the blood vessels popping in his eyes.

'I do know how love feels, Virginia, yes, but I had the sense to fall for someone suitable.'

'Suitable!' Ginny screeched, throwing her hands in the air at the hated word, all attempt at reasonable debate gone. 'I'm sick of "suitable". What's "suitable"? Edward is intelligent and funny and lively and interesting. He's has plans for his life and he works hard to make them happen. He has a big, happy family and he knows his duty by them. What more do you want from a man, Father? What difference does having a country estate and a fancy education make?'

'Several hundred pounds a year, Virginia, and if you can't see that you're not the intelligent woman I've taken you for all these years.'

'I *am* that woman, Father, and I work for you and I can continue to work for you.'

'And support your husband?'

'No! Edward can work for you too. He'd be a real asset to Marcombe's, I know he would. He's got more brains than ten of Nathan.'

Josiah's eyes narrowed.

'Don't you insult your brother-in-law to be. If you'd had any sense it would be you with the guest lists and the pretty dresses, Ginny, not your sister.'

'Sense? There's no sense in all this. I don't care about pretty dresses, and if you don't know that by now then I don't know what more I can say. I'm sorry I wasn't the son you wanted, but I've done my best and can do no more. I very much hope you enjoy your evening with Nathan, but if you would excuse me . . .'

Ginny didn't wait for permission. She fled the room, her heart racing with rage, and disappointment pounding in her veins. She heard her father calling after her but could take no more. Running up the stairs to her bedroom, she jammed her door shut and flung herself on her bed, bitter tears soaking into her pillow at the injustice of the insular, restricted little world she was forced to live in. Perhaps, she thought, glancing around her beautiful prison of a room, elopement would be the best option after all. She pictured Edward, her Edward, standing at the altar and her heart leapt with dangerous joy. But did she dare?

Edward looked up at the spire of All Hallows Church casting a shadow across their sorrowful little procession and shivered. This should not be happening. They should be here to christen little Percy, everyone decked out in their finest clothes to celebrate the joy of a new life, instead of huddled in their solemn Sunday wear to mark the loss of one. He shifted awkwardly, his very shoulders aware that they could not even lift the body of his dearest friend to mark his passing. Perry was somewhere at the bottom of a far-off sea having fought a far-off war he had never wanted to join and poor, poor Sophie was left here to bear it alone.

He pulled her arm in tighter against his body as if he could somehow make it right. She looked beautiful in grief. The days of weeping had given way to a strange, ethereal calm and she was carrying herself with a quiet inner strength that made Edward want to cry for pity and admiration. How proud Perry would be of his wife if he could see her now, but he could not, nor ever would again and that was something they all had to deal with.

'Are you ready?' he whispered, as the vicar came to the church door.

'I'm ready. In truth, I feel as if I've been ready from the very minute they bundled him on to that ship. We were too happy together.'

'Don't say that, Sophie. It's not true. There's no such thing as *too* happy.'

'You really think that? Love is hardly working out for you either, is it, Ned?'

'I . . .'

But the organ was playing now, its sombre notes drifting out into the warm air and pulling them all, piper-like, into the darkness of the church and he could say no more. His mind, however, was racing.

Perhaps Sophie was right, he thought, as he led her slowly up the aisle for the memorial service of the man they'd both loved. Perhaps too much love was dangerous. Look at Ginny trapped in her own home for his sake and for what – a life that might suit neither of them anyway? He glanced back and saw Lucy behind him, carefully holding baby Percy. She looked up and their eyes met each other, bitterness forgotten in shared sorrow, but Matthew, the fishmonger's boy was hovering protectively at her side now and that chance was gone.

They reached the front pew and Edward ushered Sophie in before him. She half smiled and he instinctively leant over to kiss her cheek. Perhaps – in time – he could marry Sophie. That would be the decent thing to do. He could care for her and little Percy and maybe give him half brothers and sisters to grow up with. He'd be no substitute for his friend, but then Sophie would be no substitute for Ginny either but at least they could live in comfort and calm and—

No! Edward shook his head making the vicar jump. He blushed in shame but could not disguise the feeling that had driven the action. He did not want to compromise either himself or Sophie in that way. She deserved to be loved wholeheartedly and surely, somehow, so did he.

'Dearly beloved . . .' the vicar began and, dipping his head low, Edward felt tears begin to fall for his lost friend, for the young widow at his side, for their child and – ashamed as he was to admit it – for himself.

As the service progressed and Perry's poor lost soul was blessed unto eternity his shoulders sank towards the rough wooden floor of the little church. He'd never felt more lonely than at this moment. He had no idea where to go from here and it was almost a relief when, through the open church door, he heard the ruthless summons of a fire bell.

'Will you be stuck in here forever, Ginny?'

Ginny ruffled her little sister's hair and grimaced.

'It feels that way at the moment, Charlie.'

'I'm sorry you're sad, Gin, but I'm glad you're here, otherwise I'd have to have Martha put me to bed and she's horrid. She scrubs really hard with the face cloth and never reads me stories. She says I can read them myself.'

'And so you can, young lady.'

'Yes, but it's such hard work that way. You read them much better than me. Can we have another one?'

'Charlotte, it's late . . .'

'Not that late. I can hear people outside.'

'Can you?'

Ginny listened and sure enough there did seem to be something going on in the street, but then it was a beautiful night. The August sun was still shining – she could feel the warmth even in here – and all those not trapped inside would do well to enjoy it.

She sighed.

'It's children, isn't it? Other children who are still allowed up. It's not fair.'

'It's not children, Charlotte,' she said, closing the door to block out at least some of the noise. 'It's just boring old adults. Now come on, time to go to sleep.'

'One more story, Ginny, please? It's not as if you have anything else to do.'

That much at least was true. Following her outburst to Josiah earlier, he had sailed out with a nervous Eliza and an apologetic Mary, leaving Ginny at home with little Charlotte. The windows had all been locked and the keys removed, and both Martha and Joseph the butler, were on alert for any hint of her trying to escape. It was so humiliating and, worst of all, she had neither seen or heard from Edward for almost two weeks. It was beginning to feel as if they would never be together.

'Another story,' she agreed glumly and reached for a book but a strange noise stopped her.

'Is that someone shouting?' she asked Charlotte.

'Probably. Martha's always screeching at someone when Father isn't in the house.'

'Sssh!'

Ginny held up a finger and crossed to the door. She could still hear people out on the street and something closer. Some*one* closer – someone who sounded frightened. She pulled open the door and froze. There was a hot, musty smell in the corridor and suddenly all the incoherent noise coalesced into one horrific word:

'Fire!'

Ginny looked around her. She was on the first-floor landing and she could hear Martha calling frantically from downstairs.

'Miss Virginia, Miss Charlotte, where are you? We have to get out. We have to get out now.'

'Here!' Ginny called. 'We're up here,' but as she crossed to the stairwell she could feel the air growing hotter and when she looked down, she saw flames, like orange serpents, already licking at the lower steps.

She opened her mouth to scream but immediately clamped her own hand over it. Little Charlotte had come out of her room and was staring at her in horror. She spun round.

'It's all right, Charlie. It'll be all right.'

'Is it fire?'

'Yes, but it's right down there. We'll get out by . . . by the window.'

'But the windows are all locked.'

'We'll smash one.'

'And we're miles up in the air.'

'Not miles, Charlotte. Someone will catch us.'

She rushed to the landing window and peered out. There were many people gathered in the street. Why hadn't she listened earlier? Why had she silenced Charlotte without checking the noises outside? It looked as if the fire had spread from next door and it had already taken serious hold. She could feel the heat rising and her little sister was now sobbing at her side as dark smoke crept up the stairs towards them. Ginny cast around and grabbed the dress her little sister had discarded as she had undressed for bed earlier.

'Here!' Ripping off the wide sash, she tied it around her sister's nose and mouth before holding the big skirt roughly against her own. 'And stay low. I'll break the glass.'

'But, Ginny, we'll never get out of there.'

Ginny knew her little sister was speaking the truth. The

elegant bay windows were wide and tall but split into much smaller panes that neither of the girls would fit through.

'We have to try,' she gasped. 'Stay there.'

Rushing into her parents' bedroom she grabbed the big poker from the fireplace and ran back to the window. It was getting harder to see as the smoke thickened. Choking, she swung the brass poker back as hard as she could and brought it swinging down into the window.

The glass shattered but the poker bounced back off the strong wooden frame, making her gasp in pain as the impact shuddered through her arm.

'Stay back,' she ordered Charlotte, swinging again.

Another pane broke and both girls leaned instinctively towards the cleaner air outside but still the wood did not give. Ginny glanced behind her. The flames were consuming the wooden staircase fast. If they didn't hurry the whole floor would collapse, dragging them both down into the burning mass below.

'I don't want to die, Ginny,' Charlotte sobbed, clinging to her.

'We won't die,' Ginny promised her, though she had no idea what to do next but just then, as she struck again at the window, she heard the welcome sound of a clanging bell and made out, just down the street, the arrival of a fire engine.

'It's all right Charlie,' she gasped, dropping the poker and clutching her sister to her. 'The firemen are here.'

'Your fireman, Ginny?' Charlie asked, but Ginny, her over-exerted lungs filling with smoke, was past answering.

Chapter Twenty-One

Edward ran over London Bridge, pulling on his fireman's jacket as he went. The bells were clanging loudly and up ahead he could see his own crew heading inland.

'Hoi! Wait!'

With a final sprint, he caught up with them and joined the men pushing the big firecart.

'Where's the fire?' he gasped.

'Paradise Street,' was the curt reply.

The firemen had no breath to waste on chat but Edward could hardly believe what he was hearing.

'Paradise Street? What number?'

'No idea, but I reckon we'll be able to tell when we get there.'

He grinned sardonically but Edward was not in a humorous mood. As they turned into the oh-so familiar street his heart leaped. Was it her house? It was certainly very close but it couldn't be, could it? Fate wouldn't be that cruel.

There was a huge crowd gathered but they stepped back as the firemen ran up, all looking to this hard little band of professionals to help their friends. A woman in a beautiful lacy evening gown stepped forward and clutched at Edward's arm.

'There's someone trapped inside. We saw their faces at the window but they can't get out. Look!'

She pointed up hysterically and what Edward saw almost made him want to faint away himself. It was Charlotte, her fingers clawing at the broken glass and her cheeky little face twisted with fear.

'Ginny,' he breathed. He turned to the woman. 'Is she alone?' he demanded.

'No. No, her older sister was with her. It was she who broke the window but I don't know where she is now. You have to help them, sir.'

Edward nodded, though his heart was bursting. He turned to the other men who were standing idly around the engine.

'Let's go,' he urged. 'Get the hose out. Pull up the ladder. Hurry!'

But the foreman shook his head.

'No badge, son – look.'

Edward spun wildly round to look at the front of number 43 Paradise Street. They weren't insured. Of course they weren't! Hadn't he gone round to supposedly try and sell them insurance himself?

'They are,' he said urgently. 'I took the forms round. I know they'd signed them.'

'No badge, no hose,' the foreman said firmly. 'You know the rules, Edward.'

'But the little girl!' Edward waved wildly at Charlotte and the foreman's hard face twitched. 'We can't leave her to die just for want of a badge!'

'Rules is I have to take a downpayment if they're not insured.'

'What? But they're not here. There's two girls trapped up there and if we don't save them there'll be no payment and we'll be as good as murderers.' He wanted to scream in frustration. 'Oh forget it, but I'm going up there.'

'Edward Allerdice, if you disobey me—'

'I'm going up there,' Edward said firmly.

Turning away, he grabbed the ladder and flung it against the wall of number 43. He could see the orange glow of the fiercely rising flames behind the glass and Ginny's little sister swaying dangerously.

'Hold on, Charlotte,' he called. 'Try and stay awake. I'm coming to get you.'

Her eyes swam with smoke and terror, but, as she focused in on him, he saw a glimmer of hope.

'You're going to be quite safe,' he said as he drew close, trying to keep his voice low and calm. 'I'm going to get you out. Is, is Ginny with you?'

'She's here,' Charlotte called. 'But she's on the floor. I think she's dead.'

She broke down sobbing and sank out of sight. Edward scrambled up the last few rungs of the ladder and reached the window. Charlotte was crouching over the recumbent body of the woman he loved and the flames were only inches away. He swung his axe round off his back. Below he could sense the crowd watching, could hear his foreman finally setting the men to the pump, but all he cared about right now was the two girls just the other side of the big, solid window.

'Stand back a little,' he called to Charlotte but she was too scared to move now and sat, clutching at Ginny's still form. There was nothing else for it – he had to break the window and hope it didn't hurt them too much.

Clutching onto the thankfully sturdy drainpipe for purchase, he swung the axe with all of his might. It splintered into the frame. He wrenched it out and swung again. One strut gave way but it wasn't enough. Again he swung. He could feel the heat pouring up the big stairs even from out here and feared for the girls inside. A memory of the first fire he'd fought down on the dockside flashed into his mind. He didn't remember being frightened then, just focused on what had to be done, but there hadn't been as much at stake then as there was now.

With an almighty effort, he brought the axe down on the next strut and, to his huge relief, the whole frame gave way. Glass and wood shattered down onto the girls but there was no time to concern himself with that. Scrambling inside, he grabbed Charlie. The slightest glance at Ginny told him that she was still breathing, though only just. Was there time to save her sister first? He knew it was what he ought to do but could hardly bear to leave her.

'Edward, – here!'

He turned to see a fellow fireman at the window.

'Mick. Thank God.'

Carefully he passed Charlotte out, holding her firmly until Mick had steadied her on his shoulder and begun to climb down. Gratefully Edward spun back to Ginny.

'Ginny. Ginny, wake up. I'm here. I'll save you. Wake up please!'

Her eyelids fluttered and she squinted at him. A tiny smile pulled at her lips but it was very weak.

'I need to lift you,' Edward said. 'Can you get up?'

He placed his arms under her shoulders and lifted. Her limbs were weak and her lungs full of the wicked smoke but he sensed her responding to his touch and she stood long enough for him to get her across his shoulders. Carefully, his heart in his mouth at the precious burden he was carrying, Edward eased himself back out of the window. He felt a rush of fresh air in his own clogged lungs.

'Take it easy,' he muttered to himself. 'No rush. Just get her down safely.'

Inside the building he heard a horrific crash as the staircase finally gave way. Below him the crowds were cheering and urging him on but all he could hear was the whisper of Ginny's breath against his ear and his own voice trying to keep himself calm. He'd lost Perry to God all too recently and he wasn't going to lose Ginny as well.

It was a long, long trip down, but at last his feet hit the ground and suddenly people were all around him, trying to lift Ginny down. There was no way, however, that he would let her go now. Ordering the crowd back, he tenderly laid her on the blanket someone had provided.

'Ginny, Ginny, you're safe. Are you all right? Can you see me, my love?'

He didn't care who heard, so long as Virginia did. Behind him he was aware of noise and bluster but all he cared about was Ginny breathing.

'Please,' he begged, and then, like a miracle, she opened her eyes again, fully this time, and she smiled.

'Edward,' she murmured and reached up her arms.

Needing no second invitation, he clasped her to him.

'You're alive.'

'Thanks to you. Is Charlotte all right?'

They glanced round and saw Charlotte already sitting up and eating a honey cake, loving all the attention.

'She looks absolutely fine,' Edward said and was rewarded by a little laugh from Ginny, but now someone was pushing through the crowd.

'What the hell is going on here?'

'Father!'

Edward cringed and tried to loosen his hold on Ginny, but she wouldn't let him and besides, already the Marcombes' neighbours were crowding forward eager to explain about the terrible fire and the dramatic rescue. The foreman and the other firefighters were pumping water hard onto the flames and already they were dying down. Josiah glanced up, his face white with horror at what could have been and then he fell to his knees beside Edward, fumbling for Ginny's hand.

'Oh my dear girl, my dear lovely girl, I'm so sorry. You could have been killed, you and dear Charlotte both, and it's all my fault. I locked you up like a fool and left you alone. I didn't buy fire insurance and, and . . .' He stopped. 'Why are they fighting the fire?' he asked, glancing back to where Edward's foreman was putting out the final flames.

'Edward made them,' Ginny said, her voice hoarse but strong. 'Edward saved me.'

'Edward?' Josiah looked over at the young man as if seeing him for the first time. 'You're Edward?'

'I am, sir,' Ned agreed, trying to stop his voice wavering with fear.

'Then it seems I owe you my daughters' lives. I am in your debt.'

He held out his big, pink hand and Edward, heart in his throat, took it firmly.

'It was an honour, sir, and a pleasure.'

Josiah nodded.

'Yes,' he said gruffly, 'I'm sure. Well, enough of that for now. We can, perhaps, meet later?' Edward nodded eagerly. 'Good. Good.'

Josiah rose, leaving the way clear for Eliza and Mary to throw themselves down at Ginny's side. Embarrassed now,

Edward rose too, but his eyes held Ginny's still and he saw his fragile hope mirrored in hers. Might this tragedy turn to good somehow?

Edward watched as Josiah pumped the foreman's hand and pressed notes upon all his fellow firemen, pouring thanks on to each and every one of them and promising to buy his Sun Insurance badge the very next day. The foreman glanced Ned's way and gave him a sheepish smile. Fighting this fire had certainly been worth their while tonight. But now, with the flames out and the girls on their feet, the drama was subsiding. People were returning to their houses and the street was emptying. The foreman packed up the engine and dismissed his men to the tavern to spend their earnings.

'Coming, Ned?' he asked. 'Reckon I owe you a drink or two.'

Edward glanced over at Ginny, looking weak and weary now, surrounded by her family and by neighbours offering them beds for the night. Josiah was right back by her side and seemed to have forgotten all about him already. He didn't want to outstay his welcome.

'Coming,' he agreed heavily and walked off down Paradise Street, secure in Josiah Marcombe's undying gratitude, but still feeling very much the outsider.

Ginny awoke the next morning feeling as if someone had locked an iron cage around her chest. It hurt to breathe, but as the terrible memories of the fire came flooding back into her mind she felt nothing but relief that she was breathing at all.

'Ginny?' She opened her eyes and found herself in a strange bedroom with Mary hovering solicitously at her side. She smiled. 'How do you feel?'

'Sore,' Ginny croaked, 'but well enough I think.'

Mary nodded. 'Don't talk too much. The doctor says you must rest for a few days and give your lungs a chance to heal. They got you out just in time.'

Ginny jolted awake at the though thought of her rescuer.

'Where's Edward?' she gasped.

Mary took her hand.

'I don't know, Ginny. After we'd got you in here, to Mrs DeLisle's, Father came out to find him but he'd gone.'

'Gone?' Ginny tried to sit up but Mary pushed her firmly back onto the big pillows.

'Don't worry, I'm sure you know where to find him.'

Ginny flushed but nodded.

'Will Father meet him, do you think? He must do Mary, surely?'

'Of course he will,' her sister agreed, but her eyes slid away.

'You still don't think he'll let me marry him.'

'Oh, Ginny, I don't know. He's keeping very close, but you know Father. He's such a proud man and even if Edward saved your life he is still, at the end of it all, just a lighterman.'

'He is not just—' Ginny's protest broke down in a fit of coughing and Mary started forward, alarmed.

'You mustn't fret, Gin. Here, sip this water. Take deep breaths.'

'I can't,' Ginny spluttered crossly. 'And I wouldn't be taking any breaths at all if it wasn't for Ned. Neither would Charlotte. Is she all right, by the way?'

'She's fine. Still sleeping and no wonder. She was up half the night playing the heroine.'

'And the house? Is the house much damaged?'

'I believe the staircase has gone and much of the furniture downstairs but they seem to think it's still structurally sound and Father already has people in to look at repairing it. He wants it done before, before . . .'

She tailed off, but Ginny wasn't stupid.

'Before your wedding. I'm sure he does.'

She tried hard not to sound bitter but knew it wasn't coming out right. Mary, however, understood.

'Listen,' she said in a low voice, glancing back at the door to check they were alone, 'I've been talking to Nathan and he'd like to help.'

'He would? How?'

'He's suggested calling Edward into the business to discuss the future of shipping. He'll be there too, to smooth the way, and he says if Edward is as astute as you say then perhaps Josiah will get to see him in a different light.'

'Really?' Ginny's tired eyes shone. 'Nathan would do that?'

'Yes. Do you think Edward would agree?'

Ginny considered. It would terrify him, she knew, but her Ned wasn't one to pass up an opportunity like this.

'I'm sure he will,' she said confidently. 'You must say thank you to Nathan for me.'

'I will, but he doesn't need thanks. Apparently his own money is very new. His grandfather was little more than a market trader so he understands about making your own way in the world – not that Father needs to know that, hey?'

'Mary Marcombe,' Ginny laughed, though it hurt her chest to do so, 'are you getting devious in your old age?'

Mary flushed.

'Not devious, Gin – just prudent. Oh, I'm so glad you're still alive!'

And with that, they fell into each other's arms.

*

'How are you doing, Sophie?'

Edward crept into the little front room to find Sophie in her chair, the baby asleep in his cot at her side and Ralph stacking wood by the fire. August was marching on and, although the days were still hot there was an edge to the air in the evenings. Edward thought of his friend's wife here all alone through winter and his heart went out to her.

'I'm fine,' she said bravely. 'Ralph's looking after me very well.'

Edward smiled at his brother. No one would believe the changes the last few eventful weeks had wrought on him. He seemed several years older and had grown into a calm and trustworthy young man. He also, Ned noted with quiet pleasure, seemed very fond of Sophie. Perhaps she wouldn't be alone after all? But it was too early yet to be thinking that way. Shaking his head he stepped up and kissed her cheek.

'You wanted to see me?'

'Yes, and I'm not the only one. You're quite the hero, aren't you, Edward Allerdice!'

Her words embarrassed him, but at least there was something of her old, jaunty teasing in her voice and Edward smiled to hear it.

'Just doing my job.'

'That's not the way I hear it. This story will keep them all going for weeks – especially if it ends in wedding bells.'

'Ha!'

Edward's face closed up at the memory of Josiah Marcombe. He'd been grateful yes, but grateful enough? Edward doubted it.

'I wouldn't buy a new bonnet,' he told Sophie bitterly.

'Well, we'll see,' she said softly 'and in the meantime I have something I want to ask you myself.'

'You do? Anything, Soph, you know that.'

'Good. Then I'd like you to be young Percy's godfather.'

'You would? Really?' Edward felt a glow of pleasure and took a few steps over to look down at the sleeping infant. 'I'd be honoured, and I'll do everything I can to help you raise him well.'

'I know you will, Ned, and I'm going to need all the help I can get without Perry.'

Ned nodded and pretended not to notice the look that Ralph shot Sophie's way.

'We'll do him right, Sophie, I promise you.'

'Even if you become a rich gentleman?'

'Especially then, but I told you, it's not going to happen.'

Sophie put out a hand and Edward bit his lip and forced himself to go and sit at her side.

'Where's my optimistic Ned gone?' she asked softly.

'Up a ladder and into a rich man's house, never to come out again,' he grumbled and then, with an effort, forced himself to shake off the strange melancholy that had overcome him since he'd walked away from Paradise Street last night. 'I'll be fine. Give me a few days, hey?'

Sophie nodded and squeezed his hand, but at that moment the door burst open and Molly flung herself inside, her cheeks glowing as she proffered a letter.

'Look, Ned. This just came for you and it's so fancy. Even the paper's rich.'

She laughed but Edward had frozen, fixated on the creamy paper in his sister's hand. That was not Ginny's writing on the front. It was a stronger, more male hand. Trying not to shake – or at least not to show it – he took the letter, slowly opened it and read the contents aloud.

Dear Sir,

*I am so very much obliged to you for saving my daughters'
lives and would like to invite you to luncheon to say thank
you and to discuss some small matters of business. I would be
delighted to see you at Marcombe's Shipping Offices tomorrow at
noon if this is convenient for you. Yours sincerely*

Josiah Marcombe

'Short but sweet,' Molly remarked tartly.

'What are "matters of business"?' Ralph demanded.

'No idea.'

Ned looked at the letter as if trying to find more meaning
behind the dark words but they remained elusive.

'Is he going to offer you a job?' Sophie suggested.

'It certainly doesn't sound like the way he'd talk about his
daughter's wedding, does it?' Edward said curtly.

'But you'll go?'

'Oh yes,' he agreed. 'I'll go.'

He closed the letter and nodded firmly, but inside he was
quaking. Was this it? Was this his chance to prove himself to
Josiah Marcombe? And what happened if he failed? Right now,
noon tomorrow felt like the most important appointment of his
life.

Chapter Twenty-Two

'Now, are you sure you're all right there my dear?' Josiah asked, fussing over his daughter as if, she thought, she were an old lady.

'I'm fine, Father, really. I feel very well now.'

It was true. The pain in her chest had all but gone, although her nerves over the luncheon ahead were doing a good job of bringing it back. Josiah hadn't wanted her to come, but she couldn't stand being invalided in Mrs DeLisle's house anymore and had pleaded to be allowed to join him, Nathan and, of course, Edward in the Marcombe offices. She was hoping that her presence would help Ned, though she knew there was little she could do to tone down her intimidating father. For the hundredth time she glanced at the carriage clock on the sideboard. Nearly midday.

Downstairs the bell rang and her heart pounded as she heard someone being shown up the steps but when the door opened it was just Nathan. He strode over to shake Josiah's hand – already so much more confident with his soon to be father-in-law – then bent down to take her own. As she looked up at him he winked. Blinking back her surprise, Ginny smiled broadly. All would be well, she was sure of it.

But now the bell was ringing again and there were new steps on the stairs. She half rose in her chair but controlled herself. It wouldn't do to look too eager, but it was all she could do to stay put when the door opened and there stood Ned, looking so tall and handsome in his Sunday best suit with a determined smile on his dear face and apprehension in the back of his beautiful eyes. He glanced around the room and then, as he saw she was here, relaxed a little as he, like Nathan, stepped up to Josiah and offered his hand. It was clasped by her father without hesitation.

'Welcome, young man. Thank you for coming.'

'Thank you for inviting me, sir. It's a pleasure to meet you properly. Marcombe's is a fine business.'

Ginny smiled to herself as her father failed to disguise his surprise at Edward's eloquence. He'd been expecting some barely literate oaf, she knew.

'Mr Nathan Johnson,' Josiah managed, indicating the young man at his side.

Ginny watched happily as Edward and Nathan also shook hands and began almost immediately talking about the riverside trade they all had in common.

'And my daughter Virginia I believe you've, ah, met already.'

Ginny felt a sudden, treacherous desire to laugh as Edward bowed formally to her and was relieved to see just a little of the same amusement in his eyes. They still, however, had a long way to go and when her father said, 'So, Edward, you're a lighterman', she thought perhaps they would never get there. Edward, however, made no pretence of his trade, but instead spoke earnestly and genuinely about his working life and the insight into the shipping business that it granted him.

Before long the three men and, indeed, Ginny too, were deep in discussion about what opportunities the new docks could offer and by the end of a three course luncheon Josiah was inviting Edward to look at Nathan's new boat designs and discuss his import strategy for the following year. There was nothing in his attitude to Ned that suggested he was anything other than a promising young businessman, but what did that mean on a more personal level?

'Port, I think,' Josiah said, scraping the last of his apple pie from his bowl. 'Virginia . . .'

Too nervous, for once, to object to being treated differently from the men, Ginny rose meekly and left the room. Barely a minute later Nathan joined her outside in the corridor, his port glass in his hand.

'Your father wanted to talk to Edward alone,' he said, then, seeing that Ginny had turned a rather deathly colour, added, 'are you well? Would you like my port?'

Ginny usually avoided such strong drinks, but today she took the glass gratefully and sipped at the rich contents as Nathan fetched her a chair. For what seemed like forever they sat there, Ginny's heartbeat seeming to echo around the high ceiling as she sipped at Nathan's port and waited for the two most important men in her life to emerge.

Finally, when she thought she could bear it no longer, Josiah's voice came ringing through the door.

'Ginny my dear, I'm sure you're there – would you like to come in?'

Leaping up, Ginny handed Nathan back his glass. He grinned at her and offered a barrow-boy's salute that sent her into the room with a smile on her face.

'Virginia!' Josiah ushered her inside, wasting no time on pleasantries. 'This young man here has asked me for your hand in marriage.'

Ginny looked at Edward and longed to throw herself into his

arms, but Josiah had not finished yet.

'Yes, Father,' she managed nervously.

'And I have said that if you are willing . . .'

'Yes, Father?'

'Then I would welcome the union.'

'Really? Oh Papa, really?'

Overcome, Ginny threw herself at Josiah who chuckled loudly as he hugged her tight.

'I think it could be a very fruitful match,' he said pompously. 'Marcombe's has plans for young Edward here.'

Ginny grinned into her father's broad chest, listening to him claim the young man as his own find and then, at last, she dared to turn to Edward. Her own, dear Edward. She stepped up to him and he took her hands, drawing her closer.

'Can this really be true?' she muttered to him.

'It seems that way,' he agreed, his voice also low, but Josiah was having none of it.

'Go on, lad – kiss her. I'll get out of your way!'

And with that he grabbed the port bottle and his empty glass and headed for the door. They heard him call a hearty, 'Nathan – news!' before the door closed behind him and they were alone.

'I'm sorry,' Edward said.

'Sorry?' Ginny's already stretched heart skipped a beat. 'Why are you sorry Ned?'

'I should have asked you first.'

'What?'

'But your father is rather, well, determined.'

Ginny laughed. 'You can say that again.'

'So–' He dropped to one knee before her–'I'm asking you now. Will you, Virginia Marcombe, consent to be my wife and to make me the happiest man in the whole world?'

'Ned!'

'Will you?'

'I will. Oh, Ned, of course I will. I can hardly wait.'

And with that she pulled him into her arms and felt his lips close on hers as they could now do every day for the rest of their lives, and she felt blessed indeed.

The bells of St Mary's rang joyously out across the river as the bride and groom, flushed and happy, emerged from the church into the glorious sunshine.

'Don't they look wonderful together,' Ginny said happily to Edward.

'You sure you wouldn't have suited him better?' he teased.

'Never! No one suits me better than you, especially looking like that.'

She touched a finger to the lapel of Edward's smart new suit. He'd been working for Marcombe's for a fortnight now and Josiah had slipped him a decent 'advance' to allow him to buy some new clothes. He'd sent him out to his own tailor and was delighted with the results.

Only Ginny knew that Edward had gone straight past the door of Jermyn and Wright's and on to a superb backstreet seamstress who had made him three perfect suits at a fraction of the price, leaving him plenty to clothe the rest of his family in the finest outfits they'd ever worn. Maud, Molly and Mercy were delighted with their lacy dresses and Stephen, Ralph and even young Nicholas looked smart and dignified in well-cut suits of their own. They made a fine family and Edward was proud of them.

His mother and father had been rather taken aback by news of his engagement at first, but their son's evident happiness had soon won them over and news of his new job hadn't hurt either. As soon as they'd met Ginny any lingering doubts were cast aside. She had promised to teach a fascinated Molly all about herbal medicines and Mercy was already her most fervent admirer. She and Charlotte, both lively little monkeys, had rapidly made friends – leaving their older siblings pleased but not a little concerned about the consequences. For now though, the pair were too busy gathering up the sugared almonds being thrown at the bridal couple to create much mischief.

'Be your turn next,' Ralph said now, coming up beside them.

'If you don't beat me to it,' Ned joked, looking over to where Sophie was tucking baby Percy into the big new perambulator Ginny had insisted on buying for her.

Ralph sobered. 'I do love her, Ned.'

'I know you do, lad.'

'I'm not going to rush anything but I think she's quite fond of me too. She needs time, of course she does, but maybe one day . . .'

'For sure, I'd say,' Ned agreed, glancing to the sky almost in apology to his old best friend.

All he saw above him, however, was the sun shining down and he knew that Perry would have told him life had to go on.

'Come on,' he said, 'the wedding breakfast awaits.'

And what a breakfast it was. Somehow Josiah had found men enough to repair 43 Paradise Road and decorate it in even more splendour than before. The wall between the little reception room in which Ginny had spoken of insurance to Edward and the bigger parlour behind had been badly damaged in the fire and instead of having it rebuilt Josiah had knocked the two together to create a beautiful open room. He'd had the latest in glass French doors installed at the back with an outdoor terrace and a wide staircase leading down into Ginny's beautiful herb garden. Now the guests could mingle delightedly, drinking the finest champagne in the sunshine or in the shade of the indoors.

'Hard to believe this was all black and scarred two weeks ago, isn't it?' Ginny said to Edward as he led her inside.

She laced her hand in his, loving how safe and content he made her feel. She still couldn't quite believe that they were allowed to be together and was treating every blessed moment with him as if it might be her last.

'I'll never forget climbing through that window and seeing you on the floor,' Ned said, glancing up the fine new staircase. 'I thought you were dead, Ginny.'

'But I wasn't and here we are now.'

'Here we are,' he agreed, looking round at the beautiful house he was getting used to amazingly quickly.

Josiah had already promised them a house of their own on their own wedding, set for just under a month away, and Edward had big plans to improve living conditions for all his family. Ralph would be an asset to Marcombe's, he was sure, and young Nicholas was showing a pleasing intelligence and would really benefit from the good schooling Edward might now be able to provide.

As for the girls, Charlotte was already working on Josiah to let Mercy share her governess (God help the poor woman, but it would do Mercy the world of good) and Molly . . . Edward glanced over to where not just one but two smart young men were eagerly hanging on her every word and smiled. His sister looked lovely today and wouldn't have too much trouble finding a nice house of her own before long. Everything really did seem to be working out perfectly. But, just as he was starting to really enjoy himself he heard a loud, sneering voice behind him.

'So those are the lighterman's family?'

Edward glanced at Ginny. She'd heard, too, and he felt her hand tighten in his own. All might feel right for them but they were still fighting public opinion and were both aware that things weren't going to be easy for them just yet.

'That's them,' agreed Josiah's bluff voice. 'Handsome lot, aren't they?'

'Very,' the voice agreed, 'especially the young woman over there. Looks like she has them buzzing round her like flies. Even so, Josiah old boy, bit rich isn't it, welcoming them into the family like this? Lowers the tone rather, don't you think?'

Edward felt Ginny stroking his palm with her fingertips but still he was on edge. He hated exposing her to this sort of comment. With one fell swoop, however, Josiah put paid to his fears.

'Nonsense, Bishop. Don't be a damned fool, man. The boy's got a real eye for business – he's going to make me a whole warehouse full of money, you'll see – and he loves my Ginny like she deserves to be loved and that's what counts. Come on now, it's a new century you know! Time to embrace change and move forward in a spirit of optimism and adventure.'

'Haven't I heard that somewhere before?' Edward whispered, relaxing as his father-in-law's friend was forced to agree with him.

'I think it was on some old lighter,' she giggled and for a moment they were both back on Edward's boat, seeing each other for the first time. So much had happened since that day.

'Optimism and adventure,' Edward echoed as the old men moved off.

'Amen to that,' Ginny said.

'Amen indeed,' he agreed and then he kissed her and, linked

in each other's arms, they knew that, despite all they'd been through to get this far, their own adventure together was only just beginning.